Michaelmas

Michaelmas

BY ALGIS BUDRYS

PUBLISHED BY
BERKLEY PUBLISHING CORPORATION

DISTRIBUTED BY
G.P. PUTNAM'S SONS, NEW YORK

SBN: 399-11653-2

Library of Congress Cataloging in Publication Data

Budrys, Algis, 1931-
  Michaelmas.

  I. Title.
PZ4.B928Mi   [PS3552.U349]   813'.5'4   76-56214

To
Sidney Coleman,
my friend and this book's friend

Author's Note:

Effective assistance in a great variety of forms was given this project by A.C. Spectorsky, Carl Sagan, Jan Norbye and James Dunne, Ed Coudal, William B. Sundown Slim Sanders, Chuck Finberg, Ed and Audrey Ferman, Bob Kaiser, Brad Bisk, Don Borah, Marshall Barksdale, the presence in my mind of James Blish, and most particularly Edna F. Budrys, in that simultaneous order.

One

When he was as lonely as he was tonight, Laurent Michaelmas would consider himself in a dangerous mood. He would try to pry himself out of it. He'd punch through the adventure channels and watch the holograms cavort in his apartment, noting how careful directors had seen to it there was plenty of action but room as well for the viewer. At times like this, however, perhaps he did not want to be so carefully eased out of the way of hurtling projectiles or sociopathic characters.

He would switch to the news channels. He'd study the techniques of competitors he thought he had something to learn from. He'd note the names of good directors and camera operators. So he'd find himself storing up a reserve of compliments for his professional acquaintances when next he saw them, and that, too, wasn't what he needed now.

After that, he would try the instructional media; the good, classic dramas, and opera; documentaries; teaching aids—but the dramas were all memorized in his head already, and he had all the news and most of the documentary data. If there was something he needed to know, Domino could always tell him quickly. It would pall.

When it did, as it had tonight, he would become restless. He would not let himself go to the romance channels; that was not for him. He would instead admit that it was simply time again for him to be this way, and that from time to time it would always be this way.

With his eyes closed, he sat at the small antique desk in the corner and remembered what he had written many years ago.

> *Your eyes, encompassed full with love,*
> *Play shining changes like the dance of clouds.*
> *And I would have the summer rain of you*
> *In my eyes through*
> *The dappled sunlight of our lives.*

He put his head down on his arms for a moment.

But he was Laurent Michaelmas. He was a large-eyed man, his round, nearly hairless head founded on a short, broad jaw. His torso was thick and powerful, equipped with dextrous limbs and precisely acting hands and feet. In his public *persona* he looked out at the world like an honest child of great capability. Had his lips turned down, the massive curve of his glistening scalp and the configuration of his jaw would have made him resemble a snapping turtle. But no one in his audiences had ever seen him that way; habitually his mouth curved up in a reassuring smile.

"I think the way Limberg's reported to have handled it gives it a lot of verisimilitude. Very much in character from start to finish. Based on that, the conclusion is that Norwood is alive and well."

"Damn," Michaelmas said. "God damn."

He played with his fingertips upon the warm satiny wood of the desktop. The nails of his left hand were long, while those of his right hand were squared off short and the fingertips showed considerable callosity. One aspect of his living room area mounted a large panel of blue-black velvet. Angular thin brass hooks projected from it, and on those were hung various antique stringed instruments. But now Michaelmas swung around in his chair and picked up a Martin Dreadnaught guitar. He hunched forward in the chair and hung brooding over the instrument, right hand curled around its broad neck.

"Domino."

"Yes, Mr. Michaelmas."

"What do you have from the other media?"

"On the Norwood story?"

"Right. You'd better give it priority in all your information feeds to me until further notice."

"Understood. First, all the other news services are quoting Reuters to their Swiss and UN stations and asking what the hell. AP's Berne man has replied with no progress on the phone to Limberg, and can't get to the sanatorium—it's up on a mountain, and the only road is private. UPI is filing old tapes of Norwood, and of Limberg, with background stories on each and a recap of the shuttle accident. They have nothing; they're just servicing their subscribers with features

15

and sidebars, and probably hoping they'll have a new lead soon. All the feature syndicates are doing essentially the same thing."

"What's Tass doing?"

"They're not releasing it at all. They've been on the phone to *Pravda* and Berne. *Pravda* is holding space on tomorrow's page three, and Tass's man in Berne is having just as much luck as the AP. He's predicting to his chief that Limberg will throw a full-scale news conference soon; says it's not in character for the old man not to follow up after this teaser. I agree."

"Yes. What are the networks doing?"

"They've reacted sharply but are waiting on the wire services for details. The entertainment networks are having voice-over breaks with slides of Berne, the Oberland, or almost any snowy mountain scene; they're reading the bulletin quickly, and then going to promos for their affiliated news channels. But the news is tending to montages of stock shuttle-shot footage over stock visuals of the Jungfrau and the Finsteraarhorn. No one has any more data."

"All right, I think we can let you handle all that. I'd say Dr. Limberg has dropped his bombshell and retreated to a previously prepared position to wait out the night. The next place to go is UNAC. What have you got?" Michaelmas's fingers made contact with the guitar strings. The piped music cut off. In the silence, the guitar hummed to his touch. He paid it no heed, clasping it to him but not addressing himself to it.

"Star Control has decided not to permit statements at any installation until an official statement has been prepared and released from there. They are circulating two drafts among their directors. One draft is an expression of surprise and delight, and the other, of course, is an expression of regret at

16

false hopes that have upset the decorum of the world's grief for Colonel Norwood. They'll release nothing until they have authenticated word from Berne. A UNAC executive plane is clearing Naples for Berne at the moment with Ossip Sakal aboard; he was vacationing there. The flight has not been announced to the press.

"Star Control's engineering staff has memoed all offices reiterating its original June evaluation that Norwood's vehicle was totally destroyed and nothing got clear. Obviously, UNAC people are being knocked out of bed everywhere to review their records."

Michaelmas's hands plucked and pressed absently at the guitar. Odd notes and phrases swelled out of the soundbox. Hints of melody grouped themselves out of the disconnected beats and vanished before anything much happened to them.

The hectoring voice of the machine went on. "Star Control has had a telephone call from Limberg's sanatorium. The calling party was identified as Norwood on voice, appearance, and conversational content. He substantiated the Limberg statement. He was then ordered to keep mum until Sakal and some staff people from Naples have reached him. All UNAC spaceflight installations and offices were then sequestered by Star Control, as previously indicated, and the fact of the call from Norwood to UNAC has not been made available to the press."

"You've been busy." A particularly fortunate series of accidents issued from the guitar. Michaelmas blinked down at it in pleasure and surprise. But now it had distracted him, so he let it fall softly against the lounge behind him. He stood up and put his hands deep in his pockets, his shoulders bowed and stiff. He drifted slowly toward the window and looked out along Manhattan Island.

Norwood's miracle—Norwood's and Limberg's miracle—

17

was well on its way toward being a fact, and truth was the least of the things that made it so. Michaelmas absently touched the telephone in his breast pocket, silent only because of Domino's secretarial function.

He knew he lived in a world laced by mute sound clamoring to be heard, by pictures prepared to become instant simulacra. Above him—constantly above him and all the world—the relay stations were throbbing with myriad bits of news and inconsequence that flashed from ground station to station, night and day, from one orbit to another, from synchronous orbit to horizon scanner and up to the suprasynchs that orbited the Earth-Moon system, until the diagram of all these reflecting angles and pyramids of communication made the earth and her sister the binary center of a great faceted globe resembling nothing so much as Buckminster Fuller's heart's desire.

Around him, from the height of the tallest structure and at times to the depths of the sea, a denser, less elegant, more frantic network shot its arrows from every sort of transmitter to every sort of receiver, and from every transceiver back again. There was not a place in the world where a picture-maker could not warm to life and intelligence, if its operator had any of either quality, if Aunt Martha were not asleep, if one's mistress were not elsewhere, if the assistant buyer for United Merchants were not busy on another of his channels. Or, more and more often, there were the waterfall chimes of machines responding to machines, of systems reacting to controls, and only ultimately of controls translating from human voice for their machines.

What a universe of chitterings, Laurent Michaelmas thought. What a cheeping basketry was woven for the world. He thought of Domino, who had begun as a device for

18

"Right."

"Why?"

"Common sense."

"Reuters doesn't usually get its facts wrong and never lies. Dr. Limberg did make the statement, and he can't afford to lie. Right?"

"Correct."

Laurent Michaelmas smiled fondly at the machine. The smile was gentle, and genuinely tender. It was exactly like what can be seen on the faces of two very young children awakening with each other in the morning, not yet out on the nursery floor and wanting the same thing.

"How do you envision Norwood's marvelous resurrection? What has happened to him?"

"I believe his trajectory in the capsule did end somewhere near Limberg's sanatorium. I assume he was gravely injured, if it has taken him all these months to recover even at Dr. Limberg's hands. Limberg's two prizes are after all for breakthroughs in controlled artificial cellular reproduction and for theoretical work on cellular memory mechanisms. It wouldn't surprise me to learn he practically had to grow Norwood a new body. That sort of reconstitution, based on Limberg's publications over the years, is now nearly within reach of any properly managed medical center. I would expect Limberg himself to be able to do it now, given his facilities and a patient in high popular esteem. His ego would rise to the occasion like a butterfly to the sun."

"Is Norwood still the same man?"

"Assuming his brain is undamaged, certainly."

"Perfectly capable of leading the Outer Planets expedition after all?"

"Capable, but not likely to. He has missed three months of

the countdown. Major Papashvilly must remain in command, so I imagine Colonel Norwood cannot go at all. It would be against Russian practice to promote their cosmonaut to the necessary higher rank until after his successful completion of the mission."

"What if something happened to Papashvilly?"

"Essentially the same thing has happened vis-à-vis Norwood. UNAC would assign the next backup man, and. . . ."

Laurent Michaelmas grinned. "Horsefeathers."

There was a moment's pause, and the voice said slowly, consideredly: "You may be right. The popular dynamic would very likely assure Norwood's reappointment."

Michaelmas smiled coldly. He rubbed the top of his head. "Tell me, are you still confident that no one had deduced our—ah—personal dynamic?"

"Perfectly confident." Domino was shocked at the suggestion. "That would require a practically impossible order of integration. And I keep a running check. No one knows that you and I run the world."

"Does anyone know the world is being run?"

"Now, that's another formulation. No one knows what's in the hearts of men. But if anyone's thinking that way, it's never been communicated. Except, just possibly, face to face."

"Which is meaningless until concerted action results. And that would require communication, and you'd pick it up. That's one comfort, anyway." He was again looking out at night-softened Manhattan, which rose like a crystallographer's dream of Atlantis out of a lighted haze. "Probably meaningless," Michaelmas said softly.

There was another silence from the machine. "Tell me. . . ."

"Anything."

"Why do you ask that in connection with your previous set of questions?"

Michaelmas's eyes twinkled as they often did when he found Domino trying to grapple with intuition. But not all of his customary insouciance endured through his reply. "Be-. cause we have just discovered that the very great Nils Hannes Limberg is a fraud and a henchman. That is a sad and significant thing. And because Norwood was as dead as yesterday. He was a nice young man with high, specialized qualifications no higher than those of the man who replaced him, and there was never anything secret or marvelous about him or you would have told me long ago. If we could have saved him, we would have. But there's nothing either you or I can do about a stuck valve over the Mediterranean, and frankly I'm just as glad there's some responsibility I don't have to take. If we could have gotten him back at the time, I would have been delighted. But he had a fatal accident, and the world has gone on."

Michaelmas was not smiling at all. "It's no longer Colonel Norwood's time. The dead must not rise—they undermine everything their dying created. Resurrecting Norwood is an attempt to cancel history. I can't allow that, any more than any other human being would. And so all of this is a challenge to me. I was concerned that it might be a deliberate trap."

He turned his face upward. That brought stars and several planets into his line of vision. "Something out there's unhappy with history. That means it's unhappy with what I've done. Something out there is trying to change history. That means it's groping toward me."

Michaelmas scratched his head. "Of course, you say it

doesn't know it's got one specific man to contend with. It may think it only has some seven billion people to push around. But one of these days, it'll realize. I'm afraid it's smarter than you and I."

With asperity, Domino said: "Would you like a critique of the nonsequential assumptions in that set? As one example, you have no basis for that final evaluation. Your and my combined intellectual resources—"

"Domino, never try to reason with a man who can see the blade swinging for his head." He cocked that head again, Michaelmas did, and his wide, ugly face was quite elfin. "I'll have to think of something. Afterward, you can make common sense of it." He began to walk around, his square torso tilted forward from his broad hips. He made funny, soft, explosive humming noises with his mouth and throat, his cheeks throbbing, and the sound of a drum and recorder followed wherever he strolled.

Two

"Well, I think I should be frightened," Michaelmas told Domino as he moved about the kitchen premises preparing his evening meal. The chopped onions simmering in their wine sauce were softening toward a nice degree of tenderness, but the sauce itself was bubbling too urgently, and might turn gluey. He picked up the pan and shook it gently while passing it back and forth six inches above the flame. The filet of beef was browning quite well in its own skillet, yielding sensuously as he nudged it with his fork.

"You don't grow an established personality from scratch," Michaelmas said. "An artificial infant, now ... why not? I'll give Limberg that; he could do it. Or he could grow a clone identical with an adult Norwood. But he's never had occasion to get tissue from the original, has he? And there's no way to create a grown man with thirty-odd years behind him. Oh, no. That I won't give him. And I tell you he would have had to do it from scratch because Norwood never crashed anywhere near that sanatorium. Strictly speaking, he never crashed at all—he vaporized. So Limberg would have had to build this entire person by retrieving data alone. But I don't think there's any recording system complete enough, or one with Norwood entered in it if there were."

"Norwood and Limberg never met. There is no record of any transmission of Norwood cell samples to any depository. No present system will permit complete biological and experiential reconstruction from data alone."

"And there you are," Michaelmas said. "Simplest thing in the world." He worked a dab of sauce between thumb and forefinger and then tasted them with satisfaction. He set the pan down on the shut-off burner, put a lid on it, and turned toward the table where the little machine lay with its pilot lamps mostly quiescent but sparkling with reflected room light.

"You don't fake an astronaut," he said to it. "Even in this culture they're unique for the degree to which their response characteristics are known and studied. Limberg wouldn't try to get away with it. He's brought the real Colonel Norwood back to life. *But* he hasn't done it using any of the techniques and discoveries he's announced over the years. Limberg's career, his public image, everything—it's all reduced simply to something useful as a cover for the type of action he's taken now. It really is all very clear, Domino, if you disregard that balderdash about Norwood's surviving the explosion. Think about it, now."

He was patient and encouraging. In the same way, he had often led the tongue-tied and confused through hundreds of vivacious interviews, making and wrecking policies and careers before huge audiences.

The reply through the machine was equally patient but without forbearance:

"Doctor Limberg is a first-rate genius—"

Michaelmas smiled shyly and mercilessly but did not interrupt.

"—who could not possibly be living a double life. Even given a rate of progress so phenomenal that he could develop his overt reputation and still secretly pursue some entirely different line, there are insurmountable practical objections."

"Oh, yeah? Name some." The sauce hissed ebulliently as it made contact with the beef skillet. A few dextrous turns of Michaelmas's fork enveloped the filet in just properly glutinous flavoring, and then he was able to place his dinner on its warmed, waiting dish and bring it to the place he had laid in the dining aspect. He poured a glassful of wine that had been breathing in its wicker server, and sat down to partake of his meal.

"One," Domino said. "He is a gruff saint, in the manner developed by many world intellectual figures since the communications revolution. The more fiercely he objects to intrusions on his elevated processes of thought and his working methods, the more persistently the news media attempt to discover what he's doing now. One of the standard methods of information tap is to keep careful account of everything shipped to him. You'll recall this is how Science News Service deduced his interest in plasmids from his purchase of olephages. As a direct result, several wise investors in the appropriate manufacturing concerns were rewarded when Limberg made the announcements

27

leading to his earlier prize. Since then, naturally, there are scores of inferential inventories being run on his purchases and wastage. His overt researches account for all of it."

"One of the inventories being yours." Michaelmas chuckled over his fork. "Go on."

"Two. All analyses of the genius personality, however it may be masked, show that this sort of individual cannot be other-directed over any significant period of time. You're hypothesizing that this excellent mind has been participating for years in a gross deception upon the world. This cannot be true. If that had been his original purpose, he would have grown away from it and rebelled catastrophically as his cover career began to assume genuine importance and direction. You can't oppose a dynamic—and I shouldn't be quoting your own basics back to you," Domino chided, and then went on remorselessly:

"And exactly so, if he'd been approached recently for the same purpose, he would have refused. He would have died— more meaningfully, he would have undergone any form of emotional or physical pain—rather than submit. The genius mind is inevitably and fluently egocentric. Any attempt to tamper with its plans for itself—well, putting it more conventionally, any attempt to tamper with its compulsive career— would be equivalent to a threat of extinction. That would be unacceptable."

Michaelmas was smiling in approval through the marching words, and pouring himself another glass of wine. "Quite right. Now let's just assume that Herr Doktor Professor N. Hannes Limberg, life scientist, is a merely smart man, with a good library and access to a service that can supply a technique for making people."

There was a perceptible pause. With benevolent interest, Michaelmas watched the not quite random pattern of rip-

28

pling lights on the ostensible machine's surface. Behind him, the apartment services were washing and storing his kitchenware. There was the usual music, faint in view of the entertainment center's awareness, through Domino, that there was a discussion going on. It had all the ingredients of a most pleasant evening, early poetry forgotten.

"Hmm," Domino said. "Assuming you're aware of the detail discontinuities in your exact statement and were simply leapfrogging them . . . Well, yes, a competent actor with the proper vocabulary and reference library could live an imitation of genius. And a man supplied with a full-blown technique and the necessary instruments needs no prototype research or component purchases."

There was another pause, and Domino went on with obvious reluctance to voice the obvious.

"However, there has to be a pre-existing body of knowledge to supply the library, the equipment, and the undetected system for delivering these things. Practically, such an armamentarium could arise only from a fully developed society that has been in existence at least since Limberg's undergraduate days. No such society exists on Earth. The entire Solar System is clearly devoid of other intelligent life. Therefore, no such society exists within the ken of the human race."

"But perhaps not beyond the reach of its predictable intentions," Michaelmas said. "Well, I assume you've been screening contract offers in connection with the Norwood item?"

"Yes. You've had a number of calls from various networks and syndicates. I've sold the byline prose rights. I'm holding three spoken-word offers for your decision. The remainder were outside your standards."

"Sign me for the one that offers me the most latitude for

the money. I don't want someone thinking he's bought the right to control my movements. And tap into the UNAC management dynamic—edit a couple of interoffice memos as they go by. Stir up some generalized concern over Papashvilly's health and safety. Where is he, by the way?"

"Star Control. He's asleep, or at least his phone hasn't been in use lately and his room services are drawing minimum power but showing some human-equivalent consumption. UNAC's apparently decided not to disturb him unless they have to."

"Are you saying the electronic configuration of his room is *exactly* the same as on previous occasions when you've known him to be in it asleep?"

"Yes. Yes, of course. He's in there, and he's sleeping."

"Thank you. I want us to always be exact with each other on points like that. Limberg's masters have taken a magnificent stride, but I don't see why my admiration has to blind me. I'm not Fate, after all."

Three

He went down through the building security systems and to the taxi dock. The dock was ribbed in pale brownish concrete, lit by blue overheads. Technically, the air was totally self-contained, screened, and filtered. But the quality was not to apartment standards; the dock represented a large, unbroken volume that had needed more ducts and fans than the construction budget could reasonably allow. There was a sense of echoing desolation, and of distant hot winds.

He saw the taxi stopped at the portal. Because the driver had his eyes on him, he actually took out his phone and established ID between the cab, himself, and the building. Putting the phone away, he shook his head. "We ought to be able to do better than this," he said to Domino.

"One step at a time," his companion replied. "We do

what we can with the projects we can find to push. Do you remember what this neighborhood used to be like?"

"Livelier," Michaelmas said with a trace of wistfulness.

The driver recognized him on the way out to the airport and said: "S'pose you're on your way over to find out if Walt Norwood's really okay?" The airline gate chief said: "I'm looking forward to your interviews with Colonel Norwood and Dr. Limberg. I never trust any of your competitors, Mr. Michaelmas." The stewardess who seated him was a lovely young lady whose eyes misted as she wondered if it was true about Norwood. For each of them, and for those fellow passengers who got up the courage to speak to him, he had disarming smiles and interested replies which somehow took away some of the intrusion of his holding up his machine to catch their faces and words. As they spoke to him, knowing that they might be part of a program, he admired them.

For him, it didn't seem an easy thing for a human being to react naturally when his most fleeting response was being captured like a dragonfly in amber. When he had first decided that the thing to do was to be a newsman, he had also clearly seen an essential indecency in freezing a smile forever or preventing the effacement of a tear. He had been a long time getting sufficiently over that feeling to be good at his work. Gradually he had come to understand that they trusted him enough not to mind his borrowing little bits of their souls. From this, he got a wordless feeling that somehow prevented him from botching them up.

He reflected, too, that the gate chief had blown his chance to see himself on network time by confining his remarks to compliments. This touched the part of him that could not leave irony alone.

So for Michaelmas his excursion out through the night-bare streets, and on board the rather small transatlantic aircraft with its short passenger list, was a plunge into refreshment. Although he recognized his shortcomings and unrealized accomplishments every step of the way.

He settled into the lounge with a smile of well-being. His tapering fingers curled pleasurably around a Negroni soon after the plane had completed its initial bound into the thinner reaches of the sky. He gazed around him as if he expected something new and wonderful to pop into his ken at any moment. He behaved as if a cruising speed of twenty-five hundred miles per hour in a thin-skinned pressurized device were exactly what Man had always been yearning for.

Down among the tail seats were two men in New York tailored suits who had come running aboard at the last moment. One of them was flashing press credentials and a broad masculine smile at the stewardess guarding the tourist-class barrier. Even at the length of the plane's cabin, Michaelmas could recognize both a press-card holder and the old dodge of paying cheap but riding high. Now the two men were coming toward him, sure enough. One of them was Melvin Watson, who had undoubtedly picked up one of the two offers Michaelmas had turned down. The other was a younger stranger.

Each of them was carrying a standard comm unit painted royal blue and marked with a network decal. Watson was grinning widely in Michaelmas's direction and back over his shoulder at his companion, the while he was already extending a bricklayer's hand toward Michaelmas and forging up the aisle. Michaelmas rose in greeting.

His machine was turned toward the two men. Domino's voice said through the conductor in his mastoid: "The other one is Douglas Campion. New in the East. Good Chicago reputation. Top of the commentator staff on WKMM-TV; did a lot of his own legwork on local matter. Went freelance about a year ago. NBC's been carrying a lot of his matter daytime; some night exposure lately." Michaelmas was glad the rundown had been short; there seemed to be no way for him to avoid sinus resonance from bone conduction devices.

"I could have told you, Doug," Watson was saying to Campion as they reached Michaelmas. "If you want to catch Larry Michaelmas, you better look in first class." His hand closed around Michaelmas's. "How are you, Larry?" he rumbled. "Europe on a shoestring? Going to visit a sick relative? Avoiding someone's angry boyfriend?"When he spoke longer lines, even though he grinned and winked, his voice acquired the portentous pauses and nasal overtones that were his professional legacy from Army Announcers' School. But combined with his seamed face, his rawhide tan, and his eyes so pale blue that their pupils seemed much deeper than the whites, the technique was very effective with the audience. Michaelmas had seen him scrambling forward over ripped sandbags in a bloodied shirt, and liked him.

"Good evening, Horse," he said laughing, tilting his head up to study Watson, whom he hadn't seen personally in some time, and who seemed flushed and a little weary.

"Damn near morning," Watson snorted. "Lousy racket. Meet Doug Campion."

Campion was very taut and handsome. There was an indefinable cohesiveness about him, as though he were one solid thing from the surface of his skin on through—mahogany, for instance, or some other close-grained substance which could be nicked but not easily splintered. From those

34

depths, his black eyes stood out. Even the crisp, short, tightly curled reddish hair on his well-shaped skull looked as if it would take a very sharp blade to trim. He was no more than five-foot-nine and probably weighed less than one hundred fifty pounds. He might readily have been an astronaut himself.

"Very pleased to meet you, sir," he said briskly. "It's an honor and a privilege." He shook Michaelmas's hand with the quick, economical technique of a man who has done platform introductions at fund-raising events. His eyes took in Michaelmas's face and form, and put them away someplace. "I've been looking forward to this ever since I got into the trade."

"Won't you please sit down?" Michaelmas said, not because Watson wasn't already halfway into the chair beside him but because Campion put him in mind of the *politesse* of policy meetings and boardrooms. He decided that Campion must be very self-confident to have abandoned his safer and inevitably rapid progress up the network corporate ladder. And he remembered that Domino had been impressed by him.

"Thank you, Larry," Campion was murmuring. Watson was settling into his seat as if trampling hay, and tilting his fist up to his mouth as he caught the eye of the first-class stewardess. "Well, Larry," Watson said. "Looks like we're going to be climbing the Alps together, right?"

"I guess so, Horse," Michaelmas smiled.

There was a pleasant chime simultaneously from Watson's and Campion's comm units. Watson grunted, pulled the earplug out of its takeup, and inserted it in place. On Michaelmas's other side, Campion did the same. The two of them listened intently, faces blank, mouths slightly open, as

35

Michaelmas smiled from one to the other. After a moment, Watson held his unit up to his mouth and said: "Got it. Out," and let the earplug rewind. "AP bulletin," he explained to Michaelmas. "One of their people got a 'No Comment' out of UNAC about some of their people having flown to Limberg's place. Jesus, I wish that girl would get here with that damned cart; I'm tapering off my daughter's engagement party. Looks like there's something happening over there after all."

Michaelmas said: "I imagine so." A No Comment in these circumstances was tantamount to an admission—a UNAC public relations man's way of keeping in with his employers and with the media at the same time. But this was twice, now, in this brief conversation, that Horse Watson had hinted for reassurance.

"You buy this story?" Watson asked now, doing it again.

Michaelmas nodded. He understood that all Watson thought he was doing was passing the time. "I don't think Reuters blows very many," he said.

"Me too, I guess. You have time to pick up any crowd reaction?"

"Some. It's all hopeful." And now, trading back for the relay of the AP bulletin, Michaelmas said: "Did you pick up the Gately comment?" When Watson shook his head, Michaelmas smiled mischievously and held up his machine. He switched on a component that imitated the sound of spinning tape reels. "I—ah—collected it from CBS in my cab. It's public domain anyway. Here it is," he said as the pilot lights went through an off-on sequence and then held steady as he pressed the switch again.

Will Gately was United States Assistant Secretary of Defense for Astronautics, and a former astronaut. Always lobbying for his own emotions, he was the perfect man for a job the administration had tacitly committed to ineptitude. "The wave of public jubilation at this unconfirmed report," his voice said, "may be premature. It may be dampened tomorrow by the cold light of disappointment. But tonight, at least, America goes to bed exhilarated. Tonight, America remembers its own."

Watson's belly shook. "And tomorrow Russia reminds the world about the denationalization clause in the UN astronautics treaty. Jesus, I believe Kerosene Willy may revive the Space Race yet."

Michaelmas smiled as if Gately's *faux pas* hadn't foreclosed Major Papashvilly's chances of immediate promotion. Especially now, the USSR couldn't risk raising the world's eyebrows by making their man Norwood's equal in rank. By that much, Gately and the Soviet espousal of fervent gentlemanliness in pursuit of the Balanced Peace might have conspired to put the spritely little Georgian in more certain danger.

Campion said, startlingly after his silence, "The good doctor sure knows how to use his prime time." Michaelmas cocked his head toward him. Campion was right. But he was also making himself too knowledgeable for a man who'd never met Limberg. "Three-thirty AM local time on September 29 when he got that Reuters man out of bed." Campion was documenting his point. "Hit the good old USA right in the breadbasket", meaning the ten PM news on September 28.

It occurred to Michaelmas that Campion realized Limberg had moved as if to play directly to the Gately-types. But Watson was missing that because Campion had made himself annoying.

"What I'm thinking," Watson had said right on top of Campion's final consonant, "is we're going to hit Berne about seven-thirty AM local. Limberg's still up in that sanatorium with the UNAC people and Norwood, and the conversation's flying. Then you figure that old man will go without his beauty sleep? I don't. It's going to be maybe noon local before we stand any chance of talking to that crafty son of a bitch, and that's six hours past my bedtime. Meanwhile, all the media in Europe is right now beating the bushes there for color, background, and maybe even the crash site. Which means that the minute we touch ground, we've got to scurry our own feet like crazy just to find out how far behind we are."

"Don't their European people have some staff on the ground there now?" Michaelmas asked gently, nodding toward the network decal on Watson's comm unit while Campion sat up a little, smiling.

"Oh, sure," Watson pressed on, "but you know how stringers are. They'll be tryin' to sell me postcard views of the mountains with X's inked on 'em where the capsule may have come down except it's got months of snow on it. And meanwhile, will UNAC give us anything to work on? They need their sleep too, and, besides, they won't peep till Limberg's explained it all, and talked about his prizes he was fortunate enough to scoff up although he's of course above money and mundane gewgaws and stuff like that. Norwood stays under wraps, and *he* sleeps, or else they switch us a fast one and slide him out of there. What do you bet we get a leak he's been moved to Star Control when all the time they've got him in New York, God forbid Houston, or maybe even Tyura Tam. You'd enjoy the Aral climate in the summer, Doug. You'd like the commissars, too—they eat nice fresh press credentials for breakfast over there, Sonny."

Michaelmas blinked unhappily at Watson, who was concentrating now on the approaching liquor caddy and fishing in his breast pocket for money. He felt terribly sorry Watson felt obliged to hire Campion for an assistant when he was so afraid of him.

"Let me buy you fellows a drink," Watson was saying. Since he knew Michaelmas's drinks were on his ticket, and he despised Campion, Horse Watson was trying to buy his way into the company of men. Michaelmas could feel himself beginning to blush. He breathed quickly in an attempt to fight it down.

"Maybe I'd better take a rain check," Campion said quickly. "Going by your summation, Mel, I'd be better off with forty winks." He turned off his comm unit, leaned back with his arms folded across his chest, and closed his eyes.

"I'd be glad of another one of these, miss," Michaelmas said to the stewardess, holding up his half-full glass. "You make them excellently."

Watson got a bourbon and water. He took off the top half with one gulping swallow and then nursed the rest in his clenched hand. He sat brooding at his stiffly out-thrust shoes. After a while, he said forcefully: "Been around a long time, Larry, the two of us."

Michaelmas nodded. He chuckled. "Every time something happens in South America, I think about the time you almost led the Junta charge across the plaza at Maracaibo."

Watson smiled crookedly. "Man, we were right on top of it that day, weren't we? You with that black box flapping in the breeze and me with my bare hands. Filed the damn story

39

by cable, for Christ's sake, like some birthday greeting or something. And told 'em if they were going to send any more people down, they'd better wrap some armor around the units, 'cause the first slug they stopped was the last." He put his hand on the sealed, tamperproof unit he might be said to have pioneered at the cost of his own flesh.

He took a very small sip of his drink. Watson was not drunk, and he was not a drunk, but he didn't smoke or use sticks, and he had nothing to do with his hands. Nor could he really stop talking. Most of the plane passengers were people with early-morning business—couriers with certificates or portable valuta; engineers; craftsmen with specialties too delicate to be confidently executed by telewaldo; good, honest, self-sufficient specialists comforted by salaries that justified personal travel at ungodly hours—and they lay wrapped in quilts or tranquil self-esteem, nodding limp-necked in their seats with their reading lights off. Watson looked down the dimness of the aisle.

"The way it is these days lately, I'd damn near have to send off to Albania for my party card and move south. Foment my own wars."

"You miss it, don't you?" Michaelmas said in a measured kidding tone of voice.

Watson shook his head. Then he nodded slightly. "I don't know. Maybe. Remember how it was when we were just starting out—Asia, Africa, Russia, Mississippi? Holy smoke, you'd just get something half put away, and somebody'd start it up again somewhere else. *Big* movements. Crowds. Lots of smoke and fire."

"Oh, yes. Big headlines. A lot of exciting footage on the flat-V tube."

"You know, I think the thing about it was, it was *simple*

40

stuff. Good guys, bad guys. People who were going to take your country away overnight. People who were going to cancel your paycheck. People who were going to come into your school. People who stood around in bunches and waved clubs and yelled 'The hell you will!' Man, you know, really, those were the salad days for you and me. Good thing, too; I don't suppose either one of us had enough experience to do anything but point at the writing on the wall. Neither one of us could miss the broad side of a barn, period. Right? Well, maybe not you, but me. Me, for sure."

"It's not necessary to be such a country boy with me, Horse."

Watson waved his hands. "Nah! Nah, look, we were green as grass, and so was the world. Man, is it wrong to miss being young and sure of yourself? I don't think so, Larry. I think if I didn't miss it, the last good part of me would be all crusted over and cracking in the middle. But whatever happened to big ideological militancy, anyway? All we've got left now is these tired agrarian reformer bandidos hiding in the Andes, screaming Peking's gone soft on imperialismo and abandoned 'em, and stealing chickens. I wonder if old Joe Stalin ever figured his last apostle would be somebody named Juan Schmidt-Garcia with a case of B.O. that would fell a tree?"

"Yes, the world is quite different now from the way I found it in my young manhood," Michaelmas said. Looking at the slump of Watson's mouth, he spoke the words with a certain sympathy. "Now most of the world's violence is individual, and petty."

Watson snorted softly. "Like that thing in New York where that freak was sneaking in on his neighbors and killing them for their apartment space. Nuts and kooks; little grubby nuts. Good for two minutes on one day. Not that you should measure death that way, God rest the souls of the innocent. But you know what I mean. Look. Look, we're in a funny racket, all of a sudden. You figure you're gonna spend your life making things real for the little folks in the parlor, you know? Here's the big stuff coming at you, people; better duck. Here's the condition of the world. You don't like it? Get up and change it."

"Yes," Michaelmas said. "We showed them the big things, and that made the small things smaller. More tolerable. Less significant."

Watson nodded. "Maybe. Maybe. You're saying the shit was there all along. But I got to tell you, when we showed 'em a gut-shot farmer drowning in a rice paddy, it was because it meant something in Waukegan. It said, 'Today your way of life was made more safe. Or less.' But you show 'em the same guy today, and it's about a jealous husband or some clown wants to inherit his buffalo. And you know it's not going to get any bigger than that.

"It's cowboys and Indians again," Watson said. "Stories for children. It doesn't mean a thing to Waukegan, except the guy's dying, and he's dying the way they do in the holo dramas, so he's as real as the next actor. They judge his goddamn *performance*, for Christ's sake, and if he's convincing, then maybe it was important. It makes you sick to think he's not interesting if he's quiet about it. Man, so little of it's real anymore; they've got no idea what can happen to them. They don't want an idea. You remember that quote Alvin Moscow got from the plane crash survivor? 'We would all be a little kinder to each other.' *That* is what you and I should be all about.

"Man, who knows what's real anymore, and who feels it? You run your fingers over a selector and the only action that

42

looks right to you is something they did in a studio with prefigured angles, stop motion, the best lighting, and all that stuff. Even your occasional Moroccan schoolteacher hung over a slow fire three days ago can't compete with that stuff. It's not like he was a Commie that was going to corrupt the morals of Mason City, or even that he was a Peace Corps volunteer that crossed some Leninist infiltrator. It's just some poor slob that told the kids something that's not in the *Quran*, and somebody took exception to it. Man, you can get the same thing in Tennessee; what's so great about that? Is that gonna make you rush out and join some crusade to stop that kind of stuff? Is that gonna touch your life at all? Is that gonna make you hear the marching band?"

"It might cause you to sip your wine more slowly."

"Okay. Yeah. But you know damned well the big stories now are some guy dying by inches inside because he can't make his taxes and who, where, has the half million that disappeared out of the transit bill? I mean that's all right, and it's necessary, and even after your third pop or your third stick, it'll get through to you, kind of, if Melvin Watson or L. G. Michaelmas, begging your pardon, Larry, pushes it at you in some way that makes you feel like you're paying attention. But nobody dies *for* anything anymore, you know? They all die only *on account of,* just like holo people, and half the time these days we just pass along a lot of dung from the lobby boys and the government boys and the image gurus like our friend the Herr Doktor.

"My God, Larry, we're just on a fertilizer run here. UNAC's just a bunch of people jockeying to get by, just like in any widget monopoly or thingumbob cartel in the world. When Norwood went, who cried at UNAC? All you heard was the hemorrhage shot 'round the world. So they shook out some expandable patsies and then they were right in there pitching again, talking about the increased effect on the goal attainment curve and all that other vocabulary they have to kiss it and make it well with. Scared green for the appropriation; scared to death they picked the wrong voodoo in school. But they're safe. They'd be sick if they realized it, but the whole world's like they are even if it would turn their stomachs to believe it.

"Christ, yes, they're safe. It's fat, fat, fat in the world, and bucks coming out of everybody's ears; spend it quickly, before the damn economy does what it did in the seventies and we have to redesign whole industries to get rich again. Smart isn't 'Can you do it, is it good to do?' Smart is 'Can you make 'em believe what you're doing is real?' And real is 'Can you get financing for it?' "

Michaelmas sat very still, sharing Watson's angle of blind vision down the aisle and being careful not to do anything distracting. He had learned long ago never to stop anyone.

Watson was unstoppable. "Norwood's up there breathing and feeling in that megabuck beauty shop of Limberg's and suspecting there's a God who loves him. I know Norwood— hell, so do you. Nice kid, but ten years from.now he'll be endorsing a brand of phone. The point is, right now he's on that mountaintop with all that glory ringing in him, but that doesn't make him real to his bosses and it doesn't make him real to the little folks in the parlor. What makes him real is Limberg says he's real and Limberg's got not one but two good voodoo certificates. Christ on a crutch, I've got half a mind to kill Norwood all over again—on the air, Larry, live from beautiful Switzerland, ladies and gentlemen, phut splat in glorious hexacolor 3D, and let him be real all over every

44

God-damned dining table in the world. Ten years from now, he'd thank me for it."

Michaelmas sat quiet.

Watson swung his head up and grinned suddenly, to show he was kidding about any part that Michaelmas might object to. But he could not hold the expression very long. His eyes wandered, and he jerked his head toward Campion. "He really asleep?"

Michaelmas followed his glance. "I believe so. I don't think he'd relax his mouth like that if he weren't."

"You catch on." Watson looked nakedly into Michaelmas's face with the horrid invulnerability of the broken. "I don't have any legs left," he explained. "Not leg legs—inside legs. Sawed 'em off myself. So I took in a fast young runner. Hungry, but very hot and a lot of voodoo in his head. Watch out for him, Larry. He's the meanest person I've ever met in my life. Surely no men will be born after him. My gift to the big time. Any day now he's going to tell me I can go home to the sixties. Galatea's revenge. And I'll believe him."

Michaelmas couldn't be quite certain of how his own face looked. In his ear, Domino had been telling him: "As you can imagine, I'm getting all three sets of pulse and respiration data from your area, so there's considerable garbling. But my evaluation is that Campion hasn't surrendered consciousness for a moment."

Watson had been clenching at his stomach with one hand. Now he put his drink down and got up to go to the lavatory. Campion continued to half-lie in his seat, his expression slack and tender. Michaelmas sat smiling a little, quizzically.

Domino said with asperity: "Watson's right about one thing. He can't hack it anymore. That was a classic maniacal

45

farrago, and it boils down to his not being able to understand the world. It wasn't necessary to count the contradictions after the first one."

It was extremely difficult for Michaelmas to subvocalize well enough to activate his throat microphone without also making audible grunting sounds. He had never liked straining his body, and the equipment was implanted in him only because he needed it in his vocation. He used it as infrequently as possible, but he was not going to let Domino have the last word on this topic. "Wait one," he said while he chose his words.

Time was when men of Horse Watson's profession typically never slept sober, and died with their livers eroded. It must have been fun to watch the literate swashbucklers make fools of themselves in the frontier saloons, indulging in horsewhippings and shoot-outs with rival journalists and their partisans. But who stopped to think what it was to have the power of words and publication, to discover that an entire town and territory would judge, condemn, act, reprieve, and glorify because of something you had slugged together the night before? Because of something you had hand-set into type, smudging your fingertips with metal poisons that inexorably began their journey through your bloodstream? For the sake of the power, you turned your liver and kidneys into spongy, irascible masses; you tainted the tissue of your brain with heavy metal ions until it became a house haunted by stumbling visions. Alcohol would temporarily overcome the effect. So you became an alcoholic, and purchased sanity one day at a time, and made a spectacle of yourself. It was neither funny nor tragic in the end—it was simply a fact of life that operated less slowly on the mediocre, because the mediocre could turn themselves off and go to sleep whether they had done the night's job to their own satisfaction or not.

Time was, too, when men of Horse Watson's profession had to seek out gory death because that was all their bosses were willing to either deplore or endorse, depending on management policy. But let no man tell you it's possible to live like that and not pay. The occupational disease was martinis for the ones that needed a cushion, and, for the very good ones, cancer. For good and bad in proportional measure there was also the great, funny plague of the latter half of the century—nervous bowels and irritated stomachs. Who could see anything but humor in a man gulping down tincture of opium and shifting uneasily in his studio seat, his mind concerned with thoughts of fistula and surgery, his mind determinedly not preoccupied with intestinal resections and where that could lead? Loss of dignity is after all one of the basics to a good punchy gag.

And time was when men of Horse Watson's profession were set free by the tube, the satellites, and finally the hologram. Now all Horse Watson had to do to pick and choose among contending employers was to make sure that his personal popularity with the little folks in the allocated apartment remained higher than most. It was a shame he knew no better way to do this than to be honest. A strong young head full of good voodoo could make mincemeat out of a man like that.

Men like Horse Watson were being cut down quickly. It was one of the nervous staples of recent shop gossip, and that, too, was having its effect on the scarier old heads. They came apart like spring-wound clocks when the tough young graduates with their 1965 birth certificates popped out of

47

college with a major in Communications and a pair of minors in Psychology and Politics, and a thirty thousand new dollar tuition-loan note at the bank.

Michaelmas said to Domino: "He knows he shouldn't say things like that. He knows some of it doesn't make sense. He trusts me, and he thinks of me as one of his own kind. He's apologizing for slipping away and leaving me with one less colleague. If you can see that, you can see that if you think kindly of him, you're being less hard on yourself. He doesn't realize he's casting aspersions on our work. He doesn't know what we do. He thinks it's all his own fault. Now please be still for a while." He massaged the bridge of his nose. He did not look at Campion. He was having a split-second fear that if he did, the man might open one eye and wink at him.

Four

It was truer than ever that airports look the same all over the world. But not all airports are located in the Alps.

Michaelmas descended just behind Watson and Campion, into a batting of light reflected from every surface, into a cup of nose-searing cool washed brilliance whose horizon was white mountaintops higher than the clouds. The field was located high enough above the Aar, and far enough from the city itself, to touch him with the sight of the Old City on its neck of land in the acute bend of the river, looking as unreally arranged as a literal painting. It was with that thought, blinking, that he managed to locate himself in time, space, and beauty, and so consider that his soul had caught up with him.

There was a considerable commotion going on at the shuttle lounge debarking ramp. Movement out of the lounge had stopped. Watson had been right about any number of details: it was likely that half the journalists in Europe were on the scene, and there was a gesticulating, elbowing crowd of them there, many of them in berets and trenchcoats, displaying the freelance spirit.

Even the people with staff jobs had caught the infection either here or much earlier, and there was the usual jostling with intent to break directed at any loosely held piece of equipment. There was a bewildering variety of that—sound and video recorders both flat and stereo, film cameras, and old minicams as well as holograph recorders—as if every pawnbroker on the continent were smiling this morning. Most of the people down here had to be working on speculation. There weren't enough media contracts or staff jobs in the world to support that mob, or, truth to tell, speculation markets either.

The current compromise pronunciation of his name seemed to be "Mikkelmoss!" and emerged most often from the gaggle of voices. Lenses glittering like an array of Assyrians, they tried to get to him in the lounge or cannily waited for him to ensnare himself among them. Michaelmas could feel himself blushing, his round cheeks hot under his crinkling eyes. He could not help smiling, either, as he discovered a staff cameraman for Watson's client network actually shooting for a zoom closeup of him over Watson's shoulder. It was Campion who raised his comm unit to block that shot; Watson had his head down and was working his way through the crowd with effective hips and shoulders.

The first man to get to Michaelmas—a wiry, shock-headed type with blue jaws, body odor, and an elaborate but obsolescent sound recorder—clutched a handrail, planted his feet to block passage fore and aft, and shot his microphone forward. "Is true dzey findet wreckidge Kolonel Norwoot's racquet?" "What is your comment on that, sir, please?" came from a BBC man down on the ground beside the ramp with a shotgun microphone, an amplifier strapped over his mouth and phones on his ears. His camera was built into his helmet, exposure sensors flashing.

And so forth. Michaelmas made his way through them, working his way toward Customs and the cab rank, feeling a sudden burst of autumn chill as someone opened a door, smiling, making brief reasonable comments about his own lack of information. Domino was saying to him: "Remember, Mickeymouse—you are but a man." As he cleared the fringes of the crowd, Domino also said: "You have a suite at the Excelsior and an eight AM appointment with your crew director. That is forty-eight minutes from . . . now."

Michaelmas reset his watch.

It was a beautiful drive into the city, with the road winding its way down to the river, looping lower and lower like a fly fisherman's line until unexpectedly the cab crossed the stonework bridge and they were in the narrow streets of the Old City.

Michaelmas loved Switzerland. He loved the whole idea of Switzerland. He sat back among the cushions with the cab's sunroof open at his request. He beamed through the tinted windows at the people going about their business in and out of the fairy-tale buildings that were still preserved, with hidden steel beams and other subtle internal reconstructions, among the newer modern buildings that were so much more efficient and economical to erect from scratch.

"The escape capsule wreckage has not been reported as yet," Domino said. "There have only been a few daylight hours for the helicopters to be out. In any case, we can expect it to be under a considerable accumulation of snow, and not indicative of anything of value to us. If Limberg can produce a genuine Norwood, he can produce genuine wreckage."

"Quite so," Michaelmas said. "I don't expect it to tell us anything. But it would be nice if I were the first newsman to report it."

"I am on all local communications channels," Domino said tartly, "and am also making the requisite computations. I have been doing that since before arranging your hotel reservations."

"Didn't mean to question your professional competence," Michaelmas said. He chuckled aloud, and the cab driver said:

"*Ja, mein Herr,* it is a day to feel young again." He winked into the rearview mirror. It was a moment before Michaelmas realized they had been driving by an academy for young ladies in blue jumpers and white wool blouses, and in their later teens. Michaelmas obligingly turned in his seat and peered back through the rear window at sun-browned legs in football-striped calf socks scampering two by two up the old white steps to class. But to be young again would have been an unbearable price.

The suite in the Excelsior spoke of matured grace and cultivated taste. Michaelmas looked around approvingly as the captain supervised the bustling of the boys with his luggage and the plod of the gray old chambermaid with his towels. When they were all done and he was sated with wandering from room to room through open doorways, he found the most comfortable drawing room chair and sank into it. Putting his feet on an ottoman, he called downstairs for coffee and pastry. He had about fifteen minutes before his

52

crew director was due. He said to Domino: "All right, I suppose there are certain things we have to take care of before we get back to the main schedule."

"Yes," Domino said unflinchingly.

"All right, let's get to it."

"President Fefre."

Michaelmas grinned. "What's he done now?" Fefre was chief of state in one of the smaller African nations. He was a Harvard graduate in economics, had a knife scar running from his right temple to the left side of his jaw, and had turned Moslem for the purpose of maintaining a number of wives in the capital palace. He sold radium, refined in a Chinese-built plant, to anyone who would pay for it, running it out to the airport in little British trucks over roads built with American money. He had cut taxes back to zero, closed all but one newspaper, and last month had imprisoned the seventy-two-year-old head of his air force as a revolutionary.

Domino said: "The Victorious Soviet People's Engineering Team has won the contract to design and build the hydro-electric dam at the foot of Lake Egendi, despite being markedly underbid by General Dynamics. A hundred thousand rubles in gold has been deposited to Fefre's pseudonymous account in the Uruguayan Peasant Union Bank. It would be no problem to arrange a clerical error that would bring all this to light."

Michaelmas chuckled. "No, no, let him go. The bank needs the working capital and, besides, I like his style. Anything else?"

"The source of funds for the Turkish Greatness Party is the United Arab Republic."

"Imagine that. You sure?"

"Quite. The Turkish National Bank has recently gone into

53

fully computerized operation, with connections of course to London, Paris, Rome, Cairo, Tel Aviv, New Delhi, and so forth. The Continental Bank and Trust Company of Chicago is in correspondence with all those, as part of the international major monetary exchange body, and is also the major and almost sole stockholder in the State Bank and Trust Company of Wilmette, Illinois, where I have one of my earliest links. When Turkey joined that network I immediately began a normal series of new data integrations. I now have all the resulting correlations, and that's one of them."

"Do you mean to say the Arabs are paying the Turks by check?"

"I mean to say there's a limit to the number of gold pieces one can stuff into a mattress. Sooner or later someone has to put it somewhere safe, and when he does, of course, I find it."

"Yes, yes," Michaelmas said. He had a very clear picture in his mind of suave, dark, blue-eyed gentlemen in white silk suits and French sunglasses passing canvas bags that rustled to somewhat rougher-looking people in drophead Bentleys by the light of the desert moon. Gentlemen who in turn paid for their petrol on a Shell card and booked air passage from El Fasher to Adana against personal checks which would be covered by deposit of lira notes which had trickled through the weave of the moneybags. On balance, if you had a mind like Domino's and knew all credit card numbers, the flight times of all airliners, and the vital statistics of all gentlemen known to engage in the buying and selling of other gentlemen and submachine guns, in all portions of the world, there was no great trick to it. "I know you can take a joke," he said to Domino. "But sometimes I do wish you could understand a jest."

"Life," said Domino, "is too short."

"Yours?"

"No."

"Hmm." Michaelmas pondered for a moment. "Well, I don't think we need any expansionist revolutions in Turkey. The idea of armored cavalry charging the gates of Vienna again is liable to be too charming to too many people. Break that up, next opportunity." Michaelmas looked at his watch. "All right. Any more?"

"US Always has learned that Senator Stever is getting twenty-five thousand dollars a year from that northwestern lumber combine. USA's Washington office made a phone call reporting it to Hanrassy's national headquarters at Cape Girardeau."

"In that simpleminded code of theirs? If they're planning to save the whole country from the rest of the world, you'd think they'd learn to respect cryptanalysis. Any information on what they're planning to do with this leverage?"

"Nothing definite. But that brings to six the total of senior Senators definitely in their pockets, plus their ideological adherents. This is not a good time for USA to be gaining in power. Furthermore, although it's very early in the morning in Missouri, Hanrassy's known to work through the night quite often. I won't be surprised if a Senatorial inquiry starts today on why Colonel Norwood wasn't immediately reinstated as head of the Trans-Martian flight. Even allowing for her intake of amphetamines, Hanrassy's annoyingly energetic."

"Better she than someone with staying power. But I think we'd better take this committee chairman pawn away from her. Sam Lemoyne's still on the night side for the *Times-Mirror*. It'd be good if he got the idea to go buy a drink for that beachboy Stever beat up in his apartment last year."

"I'll drop him a note," Domino said.

It was nearly eight o'clock. "All right, unless there's a real emergency, go ahead and follow standard practice with anything else that's pending." With the passage of time, Domino was beginning to learn more and more about how Michaelmas's mind worked. He didn't like it, but he could follow it when instructed. That fact was the only thing that let Michaelmas contemplate the passage of time with less than panic.

Michaelmas's house phone chimed. He listened and said: "Send her up." His crew director was here.

She came in just ahead of the room-service waiter. Michaelmas attended to the amenities and they sat together on the balcony, sipping and talking. She and the crew were all on staff with his employer network. Her name was Clementine Gervaise, and he had never met her because the bulk of her previous experience had been with national media, and because this was his first time with her network, which was up-and-coming and hadn't been able to afford him before.

Gervaise—Madame Gervaise, he gathered from the plain band on her finger—was the model of one kind of fortyish, chic European woman. She was tall, blonde, with her hair pulled back severely from her brow but feathered out coquettishly over one ear, dressed in a plain blue-green couturier suit, and very professional. It took them ten minutes to work out what kind of equipment they had available, what sort of handling and transport capabilities they had for it, and what to do with it pending permission to enter the sanatorium grounds. They briefly considered the

56

merit of intercutting old UNAC footage with whatever commentary he devised, and scrubbed that in favor of a nice, uncluttered series of grab shots of the sanatorium and any lab interiors they might be able to pick up. She expressed an interest in Domino's machine, which Michaelmas displayed to her as his privately designed comm unit, giving her the line of Proud Papa patter that had long ago somnolized all the newsmen he knew.

With all that out of the way, they still had a few sips of coffee left and a few bites of croissant to take, so they began to talk inconsequentially.

The skin on the backs of her hands was beginning to lose its youthful elasticity, so she did not do much gesturing, but she did have a habit of reaching up to pull down the dark glasses which were *de rigueur* in her mode. This usually happened at the end of a question such as: "It is very agreeable here at this time of year, is it not?" and was accompanied by a glance of her medium green eyes before the glasses went back into place and hid them again. She sipped at her cup daintily, her pursed lips barely kissing the rim. She kept her legs bent sideward together, and her unfortunately large feet pulled back inconspicuously against her chair.

All in all, Michaelmas was at first quite ready to classify her as being rather what you'd expect—a well-trained, competent individual in a high-paying profession which underwrote whatever little whims and personal indulgences she might have. This kind of woman was usually very good to work with, and he expected to be out of Switzerland before she had quite made up her mind whether she or the famous Laurent Michaelmas was going to do the seducing. And even if he were delayed past that point, a moment's frank discussion would solve that problem without offending her or making him look like an ass. At least this type of woman played it as a game, and took it as a matter of course that if there was to be no *corrida* in this town today, there was always an autobus leaving for the next ring within the half hour. As a matter of fact, she was the type of woman he most liked working with because it could all be made clear-cut so easily, and then they could resume what they were being paid to do.

And in fact, Clementine Gervaise herself was so casual, despite the glances and the exposition from knees to ankles, that it seemed the whole business was only a pro forma gesture to days perhaps gone by for both of them. But just before he poured the last of the coffee from the chased silver pot into the translucent cup with its decoration of delicately painted violets, he found himself listening with more than casual attention to the intonations of her voice, and finding that his eyes rested on the highlights in her washed blond coiffure each time she turned her head.

For content, her conversation was still no more than politeness required, and his responses were the same. But there was a certain comfortable relaxation within him which he discovered only with a little spasm of alertness. For the past minute or two, his smile of response to her various gambits about European travel and climate had been warming. He had begun thinking how pleasant it all was, sitting here and looking out over the mountains, sipping coffee in this air; how very pleasant it was to be himself. And he found himself remembering out of the aspect of his mind that was like an antique desk, some of its drawers bolted, and all the others a little warped and stiff in their slides, so that they opened with difficulty:

You come upon me like the morning air
Rising in summer on the dayward hills.
And so unlock the crystal freshets waiting, still,
Since last they ran in joy among the grasses.

He looked down into his cup, smiled, and said: "Dregs," to cover the slight frown he might have shown.

"Oh, I'm so sorry," she said as if she also worked in the Excelsior kitchen. It was this little domestic note that did it.

He continued to be charming, and in fact disarmingly attentive for the next few minutes until she left, saying: "I shall be looking forward to seeing you later today." And then when he had closed the door to the suite behind her, he walked back out onto the balcony and stood with his hands behind his back, his cheeks puffing in and out a little.

"What is it about her?" he said to Domino.

"There's a remarkable coincidence. She's very much as I'd expect your wife would have been by now."

"Really? Is that it?"

"I would say so. I have."

"Like Clementine Gervaise?" He turned back inside the parlor, his hands still clasped behind him. He placed his feet undecidedly. "Well. What do you think this is?"

"On the data, it's a coincidence."

Michaelmas cocked his head toward the machine. "Are you beginning to learn to think beyond actuarials?" he said with pleasure.

"It may be a benefit of our continuing relationship, O Creator."

"Long time coming," Michaelmas said gruffly. He straightened and began to stride about the parlor. "But what have we here? Has someone been applying a great deal of

59

deductive thought to what profession a man in my role would choose in these times? My goodness, Dr. Limberg, is all this part of a better mousetrap? Domino, it seems I might also have to watch behind me as I beat a path to his door."

"You are not more than part of the whole world, Mighty Mouse," Domino said.

"You know it," Michaelmas answered, kicking off his shoes as he stepped into the bedroom. "Well, I'm going to take an hour's nap."

He slept restlessly for thirty-seven minutes. From time to time he rolled over, frowning.

Five

Domino woke him from a dream. "Mr. Michaelmas." He opened his eyes immediately.

"What? Oh, I'm afraid to go home in the dark," he said.

"Wake up, Mr. Michaelmas. It's nine twenty-three, local."

"What's the situation?" Michaelmas asked, sitting up.

"Multiple. A few moments ago, I completed my analysis of where the capsule crash site must be. I based my thinking on the requirements of the premise—a low trajectory to account for the capsule's escaping radar notice following the shuttle explosion; the need to have the crash occur within reasonable distance of Limberg's sanatorium, yet in a place where other people in the area would not be likely to notice or find it; and so forth. These conditions of course would fit either the truth or your hypothesis that Limberg is a resourceful liar.

"At any rate, I called the network, as you, and asked for a helicopter to investigate the site. I learned that they were already following Melvin Watson, who had recently taken off. Checking back on his activities, I find that just before catching the plane in New York last night he placed a call to a Swiss Army artillery major here. That officer is also on the mailing lists of a number of amateur rocket societies. On arrival here, Mr. Watson called the Major again several times. Following the last call, which was rather lengthy, Mr. Watson immediately boarded one of his client's helicopters and departed, leaving Campion to watch the sanatorium."

"Ah," Michaelmas chuckled. "If Horse had only been modern enough to call the university center here and get his data from their computer. You would have been onto him in a flash." Michaelmas patted the cold black top of the machine sitting on the nightstand. He knew exactly what had happened. Somewhere in the back of Watson's mind had been the name of an acquaintance of a friend of someone he'd worked with, the man to call if you were ever in Switzerland and had a ballistics problem. The name might have been there for years, beside the telephone number of the only place in Madrid that served a decent Chinese dinner, the memory of a girl who lived upstairs from a café in Luxembourg, a reliable place to get your shirts done in Ceuta, and the price of a second-class railway ticket from Ghent to Aix. "You've been out-newsmanned, my friend. What do you want to bet Horse is headed straight as a die for the same place you've got marked with an X on your map?"

"Not a farthing. Precisely my point," Domino said. "There is more to the situation."

"Go on."

"Following an exchange of phone calls with the sanatorium, UNAC Star Control has authorized a press conference for Norwood at any time no later than one o'clock PM local. One of the men they sent in here last night was Getulio Frontiere."

"Check." Frontiere was a smooth, capable press secretary. The conference would go very cleanly and pretty much the way UNAC wanted it. "No later than one o'clock. Then they want to say their say in time for the breakfast news on the east coast of the United States. Do you think they smell trouble with more heads like Gately?" He got to his feet and began to undress.

"I think it's possible. They're very quick to sense changes in the wind."

"Yes. Horse said that last night. Very sensitive to the popular dynamic." Stripped, Michaelmas picked up the machine, carried it into the bathroom, and set it down near the washbowl as he began to splash water, scrubbing his neck and ears.

"There's more," Domino said. "By happenstance, Tim Brodzik last week rescued the California governor's teenage daughter from drowning. He was invited to Sunday dinner at the governor's house, and extensively photographed with the grateful parents. He and the girl had their arms around each other."

Michaelmas stopped with his straight razor poised beside one soap-filmed cheek. "Who's that?"

"The beachboy Stever was involved with."

"Oh." He took a deep breath. Last year, he and Domino had invested much time in getting the governor elected. "Well—you might as well see if you can intercept that note to Sam Lemoyne. It would only confuse things now."

63

"Done. Finally, a registered air mail packet has cleared the New York General Post Office, routed through St. Louis. Its final destination is Cape Girardeau, Missouri. It was mailed from Berne, clearing the airport post office here yesterday afternoon. I think it's going to US Always."

"Yesterday afternoon? Damn," said Michaelmas, feeling his jaw. His face had dried, and he had to wet it and soap it again. "Who from?"

"Cikoumas et Cie. They are a local importer of dates, figs, and general sweetmeats. But there is more to them than that."

"Figs," Michaelmas said, passing his right forearm over his head and pulling his left cheek taut with his fingertips as he laid the razor against his skin. "Sweetmeats." He watched the action of the razor on his face. Shaving this way was one of those eccentric habits you pick up when away from sources of power and hot water.

He was remembering days when he had been a graduate engineering student helping out the family budget with an occasional filler for a newspaper science syndicate. His wife had worked as a temporary salesclerk during December and sent him a chrome-headed, white plastic lawnmower of a thing that would shave your face whether you plugged it into the wall or the cigarette lighter of your car, if you had a car. He remembered very clearly the way his wife had walked and talked, the schooled attentive mannerisms intelligently blended from their first disjointed beginnings at drama classes. She had always played older than her age. She was too tall and too gaunt for an ingenue, and had had trouble getting parts. She had not been grown inside yet, but she had been very fine and he had been waiting warmly for her maturity. By the time the Department of Speech would

64

have graduated her from Northwestern, she would have been fully coordinated. But in 1968 she'd had her head broken in front of the Conrad Hilton, and then for a while she'd vegetated, and then after a while she'd died.

When he was even younger, and had to work on the East Coast because he wanted to take extension courses at MIT, he had called his wife often at Northwestern, in Evanston, Illinois. He would say: "I can get a ride to Youngstown over Friday night with this fellow who lives there, and then if I can get a hitch up US 30, I could be in Chicago by Saturday late, or Sunday morning. I don't have any classes back here until Tuesday, and I can call in sick to work." She would say: "Oh, that sounds like a lot of trouble for just a few hours. And I think I have a singing job at a coffee house Monday anyhow." He would say: "But I don't mind," and she would say: "I don't want you to do it. It's more important for you to be where you are." And he had said more, patiently, but so had she. That had been back when Domino had just been a device for making telephone calls. He had barely been a program at all. And now look at him.

He rinsed the glittering straight razor under the tap, and rinsed and dried his face. He dried the razor meticulously and put it back into its scarred Afghanistani leather-and-brass case. "Figs," he said. "Figs and queened pawns, savants and astronauts, world enough, but how much time? Where does it go? What does it do?" He scrubbed his armpits with the washcloth. "Boompa-boompa, boompa-boompa, boompa-boom pa-pa-pa-peen, herring boxes without topses...."

"I don't like it. I don't like it," he said to Domino as he put the fresh room-service carnation in his buttonhole. "These people must mean something by this maneuver with the package. What's the idea? Or are you claiming Cikoumas is a coincidence?"

"No. There's a definite connection. They've even recently opened a branch in Cité d'Afrique. Of course, that would be a logical move for an importer, but, still . . ."

"Well, all right, then. But why do they mail the package via that route? Maybe they want something else."

"I don't understand your implication. They simply don't want postal employees noting Limberg's return address on a package to US Always. Something like that would be worth a few dollars to a media tipster. The Cikoumas front is an easy way around that."

"Ah, maybe. Maybe that's all. Maybe not." Michaelmas began striding back and forth. "We've spotted it. Maybe we're meant to spot it. Maybe they're laying a trail that only a singular kind of animal could follow. But must follow. Must follow, so can be detected, can be identified, phut, *splat!*" He punched his fist into his palm. "What about that, eh? They want me because they've deduced I'm there to be found, and once they know me and have me, they have everything. How's that for a hypothesis?"

"Well, one can arrive at the scenario, obviously."

"They must know! Look at the recent history of the world. Where's war, where's what was going to be an accruing class of commodities billionaires in a diminishing system, what's taking the pressure off the heel of poverty, what accounts for the emergence of a rational worldwide distribution of resources? What accounts for the steady exposure of conniving politicians, for increasingly rational social planning, and reasonably effective execution of the plans? I *must* exist!"

"It seems to me that you do," Domino said agreeably.

Michaelmas blinked. "Yes, you," he said. "They can't

know about you. When they picture me, they probably see me in a tall silk hat running back and forth to some massive console. The opera phantom notion. However, it's always possible—"

"Excuse me, Mr. Michaelmas, but UNAC and Dr. Limberg have just announced a press conference at the sanatorium in half an hour. That'll be ten thirty. I've called Madame Gervaise to assemble your crew, and there's a car waiting."

"All right." Michaelmas slung the terminal over his shoulder. "What if Cikoumas out in plain sight is intended to distract me from the character of the woman?"

"Oh?"

"Suppose they already know who I am. Then they must assume I've deduced everything. They must assume I'm fully prepared to act against them." Michaelmas softly closed the white-and-gilt door of the suite and strolled easily down the corridor with its tastefully striped wallpaper, its flowering carpet, and its scent of lilac sachet. He was smiling in his usual likable manner. "So they set her on me. What else would account for her?" They stopped at the elevator and Michaelmas worked the bellpush.

"Perhaps simply a desire to keep tab on a famous investigative reporter who might sniff out something wrong with their desired story. Perhaps nothing in particular. Perhaps she's just a country girl, after all. Why not?"

"Are you telling me my thesis won't hold water?"

"A bathtub will hold water. A canteen normally suffices."

The elevator arrived. Michaelmas smiled warmly at the operator, took a stand in a corner, and brushed fussily at the lapels of his coat as the car dropped toward the lobby.

"What am I do to?" Michaelmas said in his throat. "What is she?"

"I have a report from our helicopter," Domino said abruptly. "They are two kilometers behind Watson's craft. They are approaching the mountainside above Limberg's sanatorium. Watson's unit is losing altitude very quickly. They have an engine failure."

"What kind of terrain is that?" Michaelmas said.

The elevator operator's head turned. *"Bitte sehr?"*

Michaelmas shook his head, blushing.

Domino said: "Very rough, with considerable wind gusting. Watson is being blown toward the cliff face. His craft is sideslipping. It may clear. No, one of the vanes has made contact with a spur. The fuselage is swinging. The cabin has struck. The tail rotor has sheared. There's a heavy impact at the base of the cliff. There is an explosion."

The elevator bounced delicately to a stop. The doors chucked open. "The main lobby, *Herr Mikelmaas.*"

Michaelmas said: "Dear God." He stepped out into the lobby and looked around blankly.

Six

Clementine Gervaise came up briskly. She had changed into a tweed suit and a thin soft blouse with a scarf at the throat. "The crew is driving the equipment to the sanatorium already," she said. "Your hired car is waiting for us outside." She cocked her head and looked closely at him. "Laurent, is something amiss?"

He fussed with his carnation. "No. We must hurry, Clementine." Her eau de cologne reminded him how good it was to breathe of one familiar person when the streets were full of strangers. Her garments whispered as she strode across the lobby carpeting beside him. The majordomo held the door. The chauffeured Citroen was at the foot of the steps. They were in, the door was pressed shut, the car pulled away from the curb, and they were driving through the city toward the mountain highway. The soft cushions put them close to one another. He sat looking straight ahead, showing little.

"We have to beat the best in the world this morning," he remarked. "People like Annelise Volkert, Hampton de Courcy, Melvin Watson...."

"She shows no special reaction," Domino said in his skull. "She's clean—on that count."

He closed his eyes for a moment. Then in his throat he said, "That doesn't prove much," while she was saying:

"Yes, but I'm sure you will do it." She put her arm through his. "And I will make you see we are an excellent team."

Domino told him: "The Soviet cosmonaut command has just covertly shifted Captain Anatoli Rybakov from routine domestic programs to active standby status on the expeditionary project. He is to immediately begin accelerated training in the simulator at Tyura Tam. That is a Top Urgent instruction on highest secret priority landline from Moscow to the cosmodrome."

Rybakov. He was getting a little long in the tooth—especially for a captain—and he had never been a prime commander. He was only a third or fourth crew alternate on the UNAC lists and wasn't even in the Star Control flight cadre. But he was nevertheless the only human being to have crewed both to the Moon and aboard the Kosmgorod orbital station.

"What do you suppose that means?" Michaelmas asked, rubbing his face.

"I haven't the foggiest, yet."

"Have you notified UNAC?"

"No. By the way, Papashvilly went out to the Afrique

airfield but then back again a few minutes ago. Sakal phoned Star Control with a recall order."

"Forgive me, Clementine," Michaelmas said. "I must arrange my thoughts."

"Of course." She sat back, well-mannered, chic, attentive. Her arm departed from his with a little petting motion of her hand.

"Stand by for public," Domino said. He chimed aloud. "Bulletin. UPI Berne September 29. A helicopter crash near this city has claimed the life of famed newsman Melvin Watson. Dead with the internationally respected journalist is the pilot...." His speaker continued to relay the wire service story. In Michaelmas's ear, he said: "She's reacting."

Michaelmas turned his head stiffly toward her. Clementine's mouth was pursed in dismay. Her eyes developed a sheen of grief. *"Oh, quel dommage!* Laurent, you must have known him, not so?"

His throat working convulsively, Michaelmas asked Domino for data on her.

"What you'd expect." The answer was a little slow. "Pulse up, respiration up. It's a little difficult to be precise. You're rather isolated up there right now and I'm having to do a lot of switching to follow your terminal. I'm also getting some echo from all the rock around you; it's metallic."

Michaelmas glanced out the window. They were on the highway, skimming closely by a drill-marked and blasted mountain shoulder on one side and an increasingly disquieting drop-off on the other. Veils of snow powder, whisked from the roadside, bannered behind them in the wind of their passage. The city lay below, popping in and out of view as the car followed the serpentine road. Somewhere down

71

there was the better part of Domino's actual present location, generally except for whatever might be flitting overhead in some chance satellite.

The spoken bulletin came to an end. It had not been very long. Clementine sat forward, her expression anxious. "Laurent?"

"I knew him," Michaelmas said gently. "I regret you never met him. I have lost a friend." And I am alone now, among the Campions. "I have lost a friend," he said again, to apologize to Horse for having patronized him.

She touched his knee. "I am sorry you are so hurt."

He found himself unable to resist putting his hand over hers for a moment. It was a gesture unused for many years between them, he began to think, and then caught himself. "Thank you, Madame Gervaise," he said, and each of them withdrew a little, sitting silently in the back of the car.

As they approached the sanatorium gate, they drove past many cars parked beside the highway, tight against the rock. There were people with news equipment walking in the road, and the car had to pull around them. Some shouted; others ignored them. At the gate, there was the usual knot of gesticulants who had failed to produce convincing press credentials.

There was a coterie of warders—a gloved private gatekeeper in a blue uniform with the sanatorium crest, plus a sturdy middle-aged plainclothesman in a sensible vested suit and a greatcoat and a velour hat, and a bright young fellow in a sportcoat and topper whom Michaelmas recognized as a minor UNAC press staff man. The UNAC man looked inside the car, recognized Michaelmas, and flashed an okay sign with his thumb and forefinger. The Swiss policeman nodded to the gatekeeper, who pushed the electric button which made the wrought iron gates fold back briefly behind their brick posts. Leaving outcries behind, the Citroen jumped forward and drove through.

Michaelmas said to Domino: "I wonder if time-traveling cultures are playing with us. I wonder if they process our history for entertainment values. It wouldn't take much: an assassination in place of exile, revolution instead of election— that sort of augmentation would yield packageable drama. Chances are, it wouldn't crucially alter the timeline. Or perhaps it might, a little. One might awaken beside a lean young stud instead of the pudgy father of one's whining child. There'd be a huge titillated audience. And the sets and actors are free. A producer's dream. No union contracts."

"Michaelmas, someone in your position oughtn't divert himself with paranoias."

"But oughtn't a fish study water?"

A little way up, there was a jammed asphalt parking lot beside a gently sloping windblown meadow in which helicopters were standing and in which excess vehicles had broken the cold grass in the sod. The Citroen found a place among the other cars and the broadcast trucks. Up the slope was the sanatorium, very much constructed of bright metal and of polarizable windows, the whole of the design taking a sharply pitched snow-shedding silhouette. Sunlight stormed back from its glitter as if it were a wedge pried into Heaven.

They got out and Clementine Gervaise looked around. "It can be very peaceful here," she remarked before waving toward their crew truck. People in white coveralls and smocks with her organization's pocket patch came hurrying. She merged with them, pointing, gesturing, tilting her head to listen, shaking her head, nodding, tapping her forefinger on a proffered clipboard sheet. In another moment, some of them were eddying back toward the equipment freighter and others were trotting up the sanatorium steps, passing and encountering other crews in similar but different jumpsuits. From somewhere up there, a cry of rage and deprivation was followed by a fifty-five-millimeter lens bouncing slowly down the steps.

"Ten-twenty local," Domino said.

"Thank you," Michaelmas replied, watching Clementine. "How are your links now?"

"Excellent. What would you expect, with all this gear up here and with elevated horizon-lines?"

"Yes, of course," Michaelmas said absently. "Have you checked the maintenance records on Horse's machine?"

"Yes."

"Have you compared them to all maintenance records on all other machines of the same model?"

"Yes."

"Have you cross-referenced all critical malfunction data for the type?"

"Teach your grandmother to suck eggs. If you're asking was it an accident, my answer is it shouldn't have happened. But that doesn't exclude freak possibilities such as one-of-a-kind failure in a pump diaphragm, or even some kind of anomalous resistance across a circuit. I'm currently running back through all parts suppliers and subassembly manufacturers, looking for things like unannounced redesigns, high reject rates at final inspection stages, and so forth. It'll be a while. And other stones are waiting to be turned." Clementine Gervaise had entered the awareness of the comm terminal's sensors. "Here comes one."

74

"Let's concentrate on this Norwood thing for now," Michaelmas said.

"Of course, Laurent," Clementine said softly. "The crew is briefed and the equipment is manned."

Michaelmas's mouth twitched. "Yes . . . yes, of course they are. I was watching you."

"You like my style? Come—let us go in." She put her arm through his and they went up the steps.

There was another credential verification just beyond the smoked-glass front doors. Another junior UNAC aide was checking names against a list. It was a scene of polite crowding as bodies filed in behind Michaelmas and Clementine.

Douglas Campion was just ahead of them, talking to the aide. Michaelmas prepared to speak to him, but Campion was preoccupied. Michaelmas studied him raptly. The press aide was saying:

"Mr. Campion, your crew is in place on the photo balcony. We have you listed for a backup seat toward the rear of the main auditorium. Now, in view of the unfortunate—"

"Right," Campion said. "You going to give me Watson's seat and microphone time?"

"Yes, sir. And please let me express—"

"Thanks. What's the seat location?"

There was nothing actually nasty about him, Michaelmas decided sadly. One could assume there was regret, grief, or almost anything else you cared to attribute to him, kept somewhere within him under the heat shield.

He watched Campion move away across the foyer toward

the auditorium's rear doors, and then he and Clementine were stepping forward.

The aide smiled as if he'd been born ten seconds ago. "Nice to see you, Mr. Michaelmas, Miz Gervaise," he said. The fading wetness of anger in his eyes gave them a winning sparkle. He checked off the names on his list, got a photocopied floor-diagram from his table, and made a mark on it for Clementine. "We've given your crew a spot right here in the first row of the balcony," he said. "You just go up those stairs over there at the back of the foyer and you'll find them. And Mr. Michaelmas, we've put you front row center in the main auditorium." He grinned. "There won't be any microphone passing. Limberg's got quite a place here—remote PA mikes and everything. When you're recognized for a question, just go ahead and speak. Your crew sound system will be patched in automatically."

"Thank you." Michaelmas changed the shape of his lips. He did not appear to alter the tone or level of his voice, but no one standing behind him could hear him. "Is Mr. Front-iere here?"

The aide raised his eyebrow. "Yes, sir. He'll be up on the podium for the Q and A."

"I wonder if I could see him for just a moment now."

The aide grimaced and glanced at his wristwatch. Michaelmas's smile was one of complete sympathy. "Sorry to have to ask," he said.

The aide smiled back helplessly. "Well," he said while Michaelmas's head cocked insouciantly to block anyone's view of the young man's lips. "I guess we do owe you a couple, don't we? Sharp left down that side hall. The next to the last door leads into the auditorium near your seat. The last door goes backstage. He's there."

"Thank you." There was pressure at Michaelmas's back.

He knew without looking that a score of people were filling the space back to the doors, and others were beginning to elbow each other subconsciously at the head of the outside steps. They were all craning forward to see what the hangup might be, and getting ready to avenge discourtesy or to make dignified outcry at the first sign of favoritism.

"I will manage it for you, Laurent," Clementine said quietly.

"Ah? *Merci. A bientôt,*" Michaelmas said. He stepped around the reception table and wondered what the hell.

Clementine moved with him, and then a little farther forward, her stride suddenly became long and masculine. She pivoted toward the balcony stairs and the heel snapped cleanly off one shoe. She lurched, caught her balance by slapping one hand flat against the wall, and cried out *"merde!"* hoarsely. She plucked off the shoe, threw it clattering far down the long foyer, and kicked its mate off after it. She padded briskly up the stairs in her stockinged feet, still followed by every eye.

Michaelmas, grinning crookedly, moved down the side hall, his progress swift, his manner jaunty, his footsteps soundless. He pushed quickly through the door at the end.

Heads turned sharply—Limberg, Norwood, a handful of UNAC administrative brass, Frontiere, their torsos supported by stiff arms as they huddled over a table spread with papers and glossy photographic enlargements. Limberg's lump-knuckled white forefinger tapped at one of the glossies.

Michaelmas waved agreeably as they regarded him with dismay. Frontiere hurried over.

"Laurent—"

"*Giorno,* Tulio. Quickly—before I go in—is UNAC going to reshuffle the flight crew?"

Frontiere's angular, patrician face suddenly declared it

would say nothing. The very dark eyes in their deep sockets locked on Michaelmas's, and Frontiere crossed his slim hands with their polished nails over the lean biceps in his alpaca sleeves. "Why do you ask this, Laurent?"

How many times, thought Michaelmas, have I helped UNAC over rough spots that even they know of? And I'm ready to do it again, God knows. And here Frontiere was counting up every one of them. Who would have thought a man would have so much credit deducted for such a simple answer? Merely an answer that would let the world's most prominent newsman frame his press conference comments more securely. "Norwood was in command, Papashvilly was put in command, Papashvilly is a major. Answer my question and you tell me much. I think it a natural query ... *vecchio amico.*"

Frontiere grimaced uncomfortably. "Perhaps it is. We are all very much into our emotions this morning, you understand? I was not giving you sufficient credit for sapience, I believe."

Michaelmas grinned. "Then answer the God-damned question."

Frontiere moved his eyes as if wishing to see the people behind him. "If necessary, an announcement will be made that it is not planned to change the flight crew."

Michaelmas cocked his head. "In other words, this is an excellent fish dinner especially if someone complains of stomach. Is that the line you propose to defend?"

Frontiere's sour grin betrayed one of his famous dimples. "I am not doing well with you this morning ... old friend," he said softly. "Perhaps you would like to speak quietly with me alone after the conference."

"Between friends?"

78

"Entirely between friends."

"*Bene.*"

"Thank you very much," Frontiere smiled slightly. "Now I must get back to my charges. Take your place in the auditorium, Laurent; the dogs and ponies are all cued. Despite one or two small matters, we shall begin shortly." Frontiere turned and walked back toward the others, spreading his arms, palms up, in a very Latin gesture. They resumed their intent whispering. Limberg shook his hand repeatedly over the one particular photograph. The side of his fingertip knock knock knocked on the tabletop.

Michaelmas stepped out and softly closed the door. "We must be certain we're doing everything we can to protect Papashvilly," he said in the empty hall.

"Against what, exactly?" Domino said. "We're already doing all we can in general. If he's taken off the mission, despite all that bumph, he needs no more. If he's still in, what am I supposed to suggest? UNAC is apparently concerned for him. Remember they almost put him on a plane for here, then Sakal ordered him back from the Cité d'Afrique airport. What do you make of that?"

"There are times when I would simply like to rely on your genius."

"And there are times when I wish your intuitions were more specific."

Michaelmas rubbed the back of his neck. "I would very much like some peace and quiet."

"Then I have disturbing news. I've just figured out what Rybakov is for."

"Oh?"

"The Russians can also think ahead. If UNAC attempts to reinstate Norwood, they won't just threaten to pull Pa-

79

pashvilly. They'll threaten to pull Papashvilly and they'll threaten to insist on honest workman Rybakov being second-in-command."

Michaelmas's tongue clicked out from the space between his upper lip and his front teeth. "There would be a fantastic scandal."

"More than that."

"Yes." If UNAC then refused to accept that proposition, the next move saw the USSR also withdrawing Rybakov. That would leave the so-called Mankind in Space program with only an East German lieutenant to represent half the Caucasian world's politics. "We'd be right back into the 1960s. UNAC can't possibly go for that, or what's UNAC for? So as soon as they see the Russians moving Rybakov up out of the pawn row, they'll drop the whole scheme. They may be rocking back a little now, but one glimpse of that sequence and they'll stonewall for Papashvilly no matter what."

" 'What' may be Viola Hanrassy and everything she can throw."

"Exactly. I wonder what would explode." Michaelmas rubbed the back of his neck again. "I would *very* much like some peace and quiet," he said in the same voice he had used to speak of darkness.

Three more steps and he was in at the side of the auditorium. It was a medical lecture hall during the normal day, and a place where the patients could come to watch entertainment in the evening. Nevertheless, it made a very nice two-hundred-seat facility for a press conference, and the steep balcony was ideal for cameras, with the necessary power outlets and sound system outputs placed appropriately. To either side of the moderately thrust stage, lenticular reflectors were set at a variety of angles, so that an over-the-shoulder shot could be shifted into a tele closeup of anyone in the main floor audience.

The brown plush seats were filling quickly. There was the usual assortment of skin colors, sexes, and modes of dress. They were much more reserved now, these permitted few, than the hustling mob at the airport.

Michaelmas stopped at Douglas Campion. He held out his hand. "I'd like to express my sympathies. And wish you good luck at this opportunity." It seemed a sentiment the man would respond to.

The eyes moved. "Yeah. Thanks."

"Are you planning an obituary feature?"

"Can't now." They were looking over his shoulder at the curtain. "Got to stay with the main story. That's what he'd want."

"Of course." He moved on. The pale tan fabric panels of the acoustic draperies made an attractive wall decor. They gave back almost none of the sound of feet shuffling, seats tilting, and cleared throats.

And out there in Tokyo and Sidney they were putting down their preprandial Suntory, switching off the cassettes, punching up the channels. In Peking they were standing in the big square and watching the huge projection from the government building; in Moscow they were jammed up against the sets in the little apartments; in Los Angeles they were elbowing each other for a better line of sight in the saloons—here and there they were shouting at each other and striking out passionately. In Chicago and New York, presumably they slept; in Washington, presumably they could not.

Michaelmas slipped toward his seat, nodding and waving to acquaintances. He found his name badge pinned to the fabric, looked at it, and put it in his pocket. He glanced up at the balcony; Clementine put her finger to her ear, cocked her thumb, and dropped it. He pulled the earplug out of its recess in Domino's terminal and inserted it. A staff announcer on Clementine's network was doing a lead-in built on the man-in-the-street clips Domino had edited for them in Michaelmas's name, splicing in reaction shots of Michaelmas's face from stock. Then he apparently went to a voice-over of the whole-shot of the auditorium from a pool camera; he did a meticulous job of garnishing what the world was seeing as a room full of people staring at a closed curtain.

There was a faint pop and Clementine's voice on the crew channel replaced the network feed. "We're going to a tight three-quarter right of your head, Laurent," she said. "I like the light best that way, with a little tilt-up, please, of the chin. Coming up on mark."

He raised a hand to acknowledge and adopted an expression learned from observing youthful statesmen.

"Mark."

"Must cut," Domino's voice said suddenly. "Meet you Berne."

Michaelmas involuntarily stared down at the comm unit, then remembered where he was and restored his expression.

"—ere we go!" Clementine's voice was back in.

The curtains were opening. Getulio Frontiere was standing there at a lighted podium. A table with three empty forward-facing chairs was sited behind him, under the proscenium arch.

Frontiere introduced himself and said:

"Ladies and Gentlemen, on behalf of the Astronautics Commission of the United Nations of the World, and as

82

guests with you here of Dr. Nils Hannes Limberg, we bid you welcome." As always, the smile dawning on the Borgia face might have convinced anyone that everything was easily explained and had always been under control.

"I would now like to present to you Mr. Ossip Sakal, Eastern Administrative Director for the UNAC. He will make a brief opening statement and will be followed to the podium by Dr. Limberg. Dr. Limberg will speak, again briefly, and then he will present to you Colonel Norwood. A question-and-answer period—"

A rising volume of wordless pandemonium took the play away from him, compounded of indrawn breaths, hands slapping down on chair arms, bodies shifting forward, shoes scraping.

Michaelmas's neighbor—a nattily dressed Oriental from New China Service—said: "That's it, then. UNAC has officially granted that it's all as announced."

Michaelmas nodded absently. He found himself with nothing more in his hands than a limited comm unit on automatic, most of its bulk taken up by nearly infinite layers of meticulously microcrafted dead circuitry, and by odd little Rube Goldberg things that flickered lights and made noises to impress the impressionable.

Frontiere had waited out the commotion, leaning easily against the podium. Now he resumed: "—a question-and-answer period will follow Colonel Norwood's statement. I will moderate. And now, Mr. Sakal."

There was something about the way Sakal stepped forward. Michaelmas stayed still in his seat. Oz the Bird, as press parties and rosy-fingered poker games had revealed him over the years, would show his hole card anytime after you'd overpaid for it. But there was a relaxed Oz Sakal and there was a murderously angry Oz Sakal who looked and acted almost precisely like the former. This was the latter.

Michaelmas took a look around. The remainder of the press corps was simply sitting there waiting for the customary sort of opening remark to be poured over the world's head. But then perhaps they had never seen the Bird with a successfully drawn straight losing to a flush.

Michaelmas keyed the Transmit button of his comm unit once, to let Clementine know he was about to feed. Then he locked it down, faced into the nearest reflector, and smiled. "Ladies and gentlemen, good day," he said warmly. "Laurent Michaelmas here. The man who is about to speak"—this lily I am about to paint—"has a well-established reputation for quickness of mind, responsible decisions, and an unfailing devotion to UNAC's best interests." As well as a tendency to snap drink stirrers whenever he feels himself losing control of the betting.

With his peripheral vision, Michaelmas had been watching Sakal stand mute while most of the people in the room did essentially what Michaelmas was doing. When Sakal put his hands on the podium, Michaelmas said: "Here is Mr. Sakal." He unlocked.

"How do you do." Sakal looked straight out into the pool camera. He was a wiry man with huge cheekbones and thick black hair combed straight back from the peak of his scalp. There was skillfully applied matte makeup on his forehead. "On behalf of the Astronautics Commission of the United Nations of the World, I am here to express our admiration and delight." Michaelmas found it noteworthy that Sakal continued to address himself only to the world beyond the blandest camera.

"The miracle of Colonel Norwood's return is one for

84

which we had very much given up hope. To have him with us again is also a personal joy to those of us who have long esteemed his friendship. Walter Norwood, as one might expect of any spacefaring individual, is a remarkable person. We who are privileged to work for peaceful expansion of mankind in space are also privileged by many friendships with such individuals from many nations. To have one of them return whom we had thought lost is to find our hearts swelling with great emotion."

He was off and winging now. Whatever Frontiere had written and drilled into him was now nothing more than an outline for spontaneous creative rhetoric. That was all right, too, so far, because Frontiere in turn had based the words on guidelines first articulated to him by Sakal. But so much for the skills of prose communication.

Sakal was looking earnestly into the camera, his hands gripping the sides of the podium. "The number of Man's space pioneers has not today been made one more. We have *all* been made greater—you and I as well as those whose training and experience are directed at actually piloting our craft in their journeys upon this mighty frontier."

Michaelmas kept still. It wasn't easy. For a moment, it had seemed that Sakal's private fondness for John F. Kennedy would lead him into speaking of "this new ocean." His natural caution had diverted him away from that, but only into a near stumble over "New Frontier," an even more widely known Kennedyism. Sakal wasn't merely enraged; he was rattled, and that was something Michaelmas had never seen before.

"We look forward to working with Colonel Norwood again," Sakal said. "There are many projects on the schedule of the UNAC which require the rare qualities of someone like himself. Whatever his assignment, Colonel Norwood will perform faithfully in the best traditions of the UNAC and for the good of all mankind."

Well, he had gone by way of Robin Hood's barn, but he had finally gotten there. Now to point it out. Michaelmas keyed Transmit and locked.

"Ladies and gentlemen," he said, "we have just heard the news that Colonel Norwood will indeed be returning to operational status with UNAC. His new duties cannot be made definite at this time, but Mr. Sakal is obviously anxious to underscore that it will be an assignment of considerable importance." As well as to let us all know that he is as concerned for his good buddy's well-being as anyone could be, and as well as to betray that UNAC is suddenly looking back a generation. Damn. Organizations nurtured specialists like Frontiere to dress policy in jackets of bulletproof phrasing, and then the policymakers succumbed to improvisation on camera because it made them feel more convincing to use their own words.

Speaking of words . . .

"A position of high responsibility is certainly in order for the colonel if he is fully recovered," Michaelmas was saying. It was gratifying how automatically the mind and the tongue worked together, first one leading and then the other, the one never more than a millimicrosecond behind the other, whichever was appropriate to the situation. The face, too: the wise older friend, the worldly counselor. The situation is always important, but neither inexplicable nor cause for gloom. "The vast amount of physical catching-up to do—the months of training and rehearsal that have passed in Colonel Norwood's absence from UNAC's programs—would make it extremely difficult to rejoin any ongoing project." Smooth. As the sentence had flowed forward, he had considered and rejected saying "impossible." In fact it probably was barely possible; with a large crew, redundant functions, and modern guidance systems, spaceflight was far from the trapeze act it had been in Will Gately's day. And if I am going to make UNAC work, if I am going to make work all the things of which UNAC is only the currently prominent part, then the last thing I can do is be seen trying to make it work. So I can't really be any more direct than Sakal was being, can I? Smile inside, wise older friend. They call it irony. It is in fact the way of the world. "It's possible Mr. Sakal is hinting at the directorship of the Outer Planet Applications program, which will convert into industrial processes the results of the engineering experiments to be brought back by the Outer Planets expedition." It's also possible Laurent Michaelmas is throwing UNAC a broad hint on how to kick Norwood upstairs. Perhaps in the hope that while they kick him, his arse will open to disclose gear trains. What then, Dr. Limberg? What now, Laurent Michaelmas? All he had beside him was a magic box full of nothing—a still, clever thing that did not even understand it was a tool, nor could appreciate how skillfully it was employed. "And now, back to Mr. Sakal."

All Sakal was doing was introducing Limberg, and waiting until the old man was well advanced from the wings before circling around the table and taking one of the three chairs. Everyone was so knowledgeable on playing for the media these days. They kept it short, they broke it to allow time for comment, they didn't upstage each other. Even when they were in a snit, they built these things like actors re-creating psychodramas from a transcript. It was not *they* who had pushed the switch, nodded the head, closed the door, written the voucher. Someone else—someone wild, someone devious, someone unpredictable—had done that. No such persons would be thrust upon the audience today. Or ever. Such persons and their deeds were *represented* here today. And each day. There *is* a reality. We will tell you about it.

Of course, these people here on Limberg's stage were the survivors of the selection process. The ones who didn't begin learning it early were the ones you never heard of.

"Dr. Limberg naturally needs no introduction," Michaelmas said to a great many millions of people—few of them, it seemed, buried deep in the evening hours. Prime Time was advancing slothfully out in the Pacific wasteland. Why was that? "What he appears to deserve is the world's gratitude."

Unlock. The great man stands there like a graven saint. The kind, knowing eyes sweep both the live and the electronic audience. The podium light, which had cast the juts and hollows of Sakal's face into harsh no-nonsense relief, seemed now to be more diffuse, and perhaps a more flattering shade. Michaelmas sighed. Well, we all do it one way or another.

"Welcome to my house," Limberg said in German. Michaelmas thought about it for a moment, then put a translator output in his ear. He could speak and understand it, especially the western dialects, but there might be some nuance, either direct from Limberg or unconsciously created by the translator. In that latter case, what the translator made of Limberg would be more official among whatever ethnic group heard it that way. Eventually the Michaelmases and Horse Watsons of the world would have to track down the distortion if they could or if they cared, and set it right in one corner without disturbing another. Not for the first time, Michaelmas wished Esperanto had taken hold. But recalling the nightmare of America's attempt to force metrication on itself, he did not wish it quite enough.

Limberg was smiling and twinkling, his hands out, the genial host. "My associates and I are deeply honored. I can report to you that we did not fail our responsibilities toward the miracle that conveyed Colonel Norwood in such distress to us." Now the visage was solemn, but the stance of his shoulders and slightly bowed head indicated quiet pride.

Overweening, Michaelmas thought. The man radiates goodness and wisdom like a rich uncle in a nephew's eyes. And so it is with the world; those who claim mankind knows nothing of justice, restraint, modesty, or altruism are all wrong. In every generation, we have several individuals singled out to represent them to us.

Disquieting. To sit here suddenly suspecting the old man's pedigree. What to think of the witnesses to his parents' marriage? *Is* there sanctity in the baptismal register? If Uncle's birth certificate is an enigma, what does that do to Nephew's claim of kinship when probate time comes round?

Better not whisper such suppositions in the world's lent ear just yet. But how, then, for the straight, inquiring professional newsman to look at him just now?

No man can be a hero to his media. The old man's ego and his gesturings were common stock in after-hours conversation. But they all played along, seeing it harmless when compared to his majesty of mind—assuming he had some. They let him be the man in the white coat, and he gave them stitches of newsworthy words to suture up fistulas of dead air, the recipient not only of two Nobel awards but of two crashes. . . .

If Domino were here, Michaelmas thought, oppressed, he

would have pulled me up for persiflage long before now.

What *is* it? he thought. What in the world are they doing to me and mine? Who are they?

Limberg, meanwhile, was spieling out all the improbables of Norwood's crash so near the sanatorium, so far from the world's attention. If it weren't Limberg, and if they weren't all so certain Norwood was waiting alive and seamless in the wings, how many of them here in this room would have been willing to swallow it? But when he looked around him now, Michaelmas could see it going down whole, glutinously.

And maybe it's really that way? he thought, finally.

Ah, no, no, they are using the mails to defraud somehow. And most important I think they have killed Horse Watson, probably because he frightened them with how swiftly he could move.

When he thought of that, he felt more confident. If they were really monolithically masterly, they'd have had the wreckage all dressed and propped as required. More, they would have been icy sure of it, come Nineveh, come Iron Darius and all his chariots against them. But they hadn't liked Watson's directness. They'd panicked a little. Someone on the crew had said, "Wait—no, let's take one more look at it before we put it on exhibit." And so they had knocked Watson down not only to forestall him but to distract the crowd while they sidled out and made assurance doubly sure.

It was good to think they could be nervous.

It was bad to think nevertheless how capable they were.

Now Limberg was into orthopedics, immunology, tissue cloning; it was all believable. It was years since they'd announced being able to grow a new heart from a snippet of a bad one; what was apparently new was being able to grow it in time to do the patient any good.

Keying in, Michaelmas said a few words about that to his

90

audience, just as if he believed it. Meanwhile, he admired the
way Limberg was teasing the time away, letting the press
corps wind up tighter and tighter just as if they were
ordinary rubes awaiting the star turn at the snake oil show,
instead of the dukes and duchesses of world opinion.

"—but the details of these things," Limberg was finally
concluding, "are of course best left for later consideration. I
am privileged now to reintroduce to you the United States of
North America astronaut Colonel Doctor of Engineering
Walter Norwood."

And there he was, striding out of the wings, suddenly
washed in light, grinning and raising one hand boyishly in a
wave of greeting. Every lens in the room sucked him in,
every heart beat louder in that mesmerized crowd, and the
media punched him direct into the world's gut. But not on
prime time. Of all the scheduling they could have set up, this
was just about the worst. Not that there was any way to take
much of the edge off this one. Nevertheless, when this news
arrived at Mr. and Mrs. America's breakfast table, it would
be hours cold—warmed over, blurred by subsequent events of
whatever kind. A bathing beauty might give birth and name
a dolphin as the father. Professional terrorists, hired by
Corsican investors in the Carlsbad radium spa, might bomb
President Fefre's palace. General Motors might announce
there would be no new models for the year 2001, since the
world was coming to an end.

It suddenly occurred to Michaelmas that if he were
UNAC, he'd have had Papashvilly here to shake Norwood's
hand at this moment and throw a comradely arm around his
shoulders, and thus emphasize just who it was that was being
welcomed home and who it was that had drawn the water
and hewn the wood meanwhile.

But they had retreated from that opportunity. Why? No

time to wonder. Norwood was standing alone at the podium. Limberg had drifted back to join Sakal at the table, Frontiere was blended into the walls somewhere until Q and A time, and the American colonel had the attention. He had it pretty well, too. Limberg's lighting electricians were doing a masterful job on him.

"I'm very glad to see you all," Norwood said softly into the cameras, his hair an aureole of backlighting. He raised his chin a little, and his facial lines were bathed out by a spot mounted out of sight somewhere in the podium box itself. "I want to thank Dr. Limberg and his staff." He was like an angel. Michaelmas's hackles were rising. "And now I'm ready to sit down and take questions." He smiled, waved his hand again, and stepped back.

The lighting changed; now the podium was played down, and the table was illuminated. Sakal and Limberg were standing. Frontiere was coming out of the wings. Norwood reached his chair. The press corps leaned forward, some with hands rising and mouths opening to call attention to their questions, and as they leaned some lackey somewhere began to applaud. Caught on the lean, it was easy to stand. Standing, it was easy to applaud. Scores of palms resounded, and the walls quivered. Limberg as well as Norwood smiled and nodded modestly.

Michaelmas fidgeted. He closed his fists. Where was the statement explaining exactly what had happened? Where was the UNAC physicist with his charts and pointer, his vocabulary full of coriolis effect and telemetry nulls, his animation holograms of how a radar horizon swallows a man-carrying capsule? If no one else was going to do it, Norwood should have.

92

It wasn't going to happen. In another moment, a hundred and a half people, each with an individual idea of what needed asking, were going to begin competing for short answers to breathless questions. The man whose media radiated its signal from an overhead satellite to a clientele of bangled cattlemen in wattle huts had concerns not shared by the correspondent for Dow Jones. The people from Science News Service hardly listened to whatever response was drawn by the representative of *Elle*. And there was only a circumscribed area of time to work in. The bathing beauty was out there somewhere, jostling Fefre and chiliasm for space on the channels, jockeying her anomalously presented hips.

It was all over. They were not here to obtain information after all. They were here to sanctify the occasion, and when they were done the world would think it knew the truth and was free.

Frontiere was at the podium. This sort of thing was his handiwork. He moved effortlessly, a man who had danced this sort of minuet once or twice before. UNAC's man, but doing the job Limberg wanted done.

And thus Sakal's impotent rage. Somehow the Bird was over the grand old man's barrel.

"The questions?" Frontiere was saying to the press corps.

My hat is off to you, you son of a bitch, Michaelmas was saying, and yes, indeed, we will talk afterward, friend to friend. I am senior in prestige here; it is incumbent on me to frame the first question. To set the tone, so to speak. I raise my hand. Getulio smiles toward me. "Yes, Mr. Michaelmas?"

"Colonel Norwood's presence here delights us all," I say. There are amenities that must of course be followed. I make the obligatory remark on behalf of the media. But I am the first voice from the floor. The world hears me. I have spoken. It's all true. He is risc.. The people of the world rejoice.

But they are *my* people! God damn it, *my* people!

"My question is for Mr. Sakal. I'd like him to explain how Colonel Norwood's presence here jibes with UNAC's prior explanations of his death." I stand with a faint little twinkle visible in my eye. I am gently needling the bureaucrats. I am in fact doing no such thing. If Frontiere and Sakal have not already rehearsed this question a thousand times, then they are *all* imposters. I am a clown. I toss the ball so they may catch it gracefully.

Sakal leans forward in his chair, his hands cupped on the table. "Well, obviously," he delivers, "there was some sort of failure in our tracking and monitoring systems." He causes himself to appear rueful. "Some embarrassing failure."

We all chuckle.

"I assume it's being gone into."

"Oh, yes." Something in the set of Sakal's jaw informs the audience that somewhere out there blades are thudding and heads are rolling.

I have asked my questions. I have set the tone. I have salvaged what I can from this wreck. My audience thinks I was not afraid to ask a delicate question, and delicate enough not to couch it in a disquieting manner.

I sit down. The next questioner is recognized. Frontiere is a genius at seeming to select on some rational basis of priority. In due time, he gets to Douglas Campion. See Campion stand. "Colonel Norwood, what's your next destination? Will you be coming to the USA in the near future?"

"Well, that depends on my duty assignment."

94

"Would you accept a Presidential invitation?" He slips it in quickly. Sakal regards him quietly.

"If we had such an invitation," Sakal answers for Norwood. "We would of course arrange duty time off for Colonel Norwood in order that he might visit with the chief executive of his native land, yes."

Ah, news. And the hero could then doubtless be diverted for a few tickertape parades, etc. Campion has shrewdly uncovered the obvious inevitable. But it was a good question to have been seen asking.

Ah, you bastards, bastards, bastards. I sit in my place. In a decent while, I will ask another question of some kind. But if I were the man you think me, the questions I'd ask would have you in pieces. Phut, splat! Live in glorious hexacolor, direct from Switzerland, ladies and gentlemen, if I were not also only a clever simulacrum of what I ought to be.

Seven

The sorry business wound itself down toward eleven-thirty. For his audience, Michaelmas ran off a few closing comments in dignity. After everything was off the air, Frontiere announced a small press reception in the dining hall, "for those who could stay." It was understood on occasions of this sort that crew technicians are too busy to stay, since it had long ago been discovered that even one cameraman at a buffet was worth a horde of locusts, and tended to make awkward small talk.

The dining hall featured a glass overlook of the depths below and the heights above; even through the metallized panes, the sun would have driven in fiercely if a drape, gauzy as a scrim, had not been hung upon it. Air-warming ducts along the wall set it to rippling. The world beyond the dining hall was beautiful and rhythmic. The press strolled from bunch to bunch of themselves and various UNAC functionaries, sanatorium staff, and of course Norwood. There was a bar at each end of the large room, and the carpet underfoot was conducive to a silent, gliding step that was both restful and ennobling. For some, stepping back and forth from one end of the room to the other was particularly exhilarating.

Michaelmas wore his smile. He took a Kirr and nibbled tender spiced rare lamb slivers on a coaster of trimmed pumpernickel. He found Norwood, Limberg and Frontiere all together, standing against a tapestry depicting medieval physicians in consultation at the bedside of a dying monarch. Up close, Norwood looked much more like he ought—fineline wrinkles in the taut skin, a gray hair for every two blond ones, a few broken capillaries in his cheeks. By now Michaelmas had downed the *hors d'oeuvre*. He held out his hand. "Good morning, Walt. You don't appear the least bit changed, I'm pleased to be able to say."

"Hello, Larry." Norwood grinned. "Yeah. Feels good."

Limberg had taken off his white duster and was revealed in a greenish old tweed suit that accordioned at the elbows and knees. A tasseled Bavarian pipe curved down from one corner of his mouth and rested in the cup of one palm. He sucked on it in measured intervals, and aromatic blue wisps of smoke escaped his flattened lips. Michaelmas smiled at him. "My congratulations, Doctor. The world may not contain sufficient honors."

Limberg's hound-dog eyes turned upward toward Michaelmas's face. He said: "It is not honors that cause one to accomplish such things."

"No, of course not." Michaelmas turned to Frontiere. "Ah, Getulio. And where is Ossip? I don't see him."

98

"Mr. Sakal is a little indisposed and had to leave," Limberg said. "As his co-host for this reception, I express his regrets." Frontiere nodded.

"I am very sorry to hear that," Michaelmas said. "Getulio, I wonder if I might take you aside and speak with you for just a moment. Excuse me, Dr. Limberg, Walter. I must leave for my hotel almost immediately, and Mr. Frontiere and I have an old promise to keep."

"Certainly, Mr. Michaelmas. Thank you for coming." Suck suck. Wisp.

Michaelmas moved Frontiere aside with a gentle touch on the upper arm. "I am at the Excelsior," he said quietly. "I will be in Switzerland perhaps a few hours more, perhaps not. I hope you'll be able to find the time to meet me." He laughed and affectionately patted Frontiere's cheek. "I hope you can arrange it," he said in a normal tone. "*Arrivederci.*" He turned away with a wave and moved toward where he had seen Clementine chatting beside a tall, cadaverous, fortyish bald man with a professorial manner.

Clementine was wearing a pair of low canvas shoes, presumably borrowed from a crew member. She smiled as she saw Michaelmas looking at her feet. "Laurent," she said with a graceful inclination of her head. He took her hand, bowed, and kissed it.

"Thank you."

"*Merci. Pas de quoi.*" A little bit of laughter lingered between them in their eyes. She turned to the man beside her. His olive skin and sunken, lustrous, and very round brown eyes were not quite right for a pin-striped navy blue suit, but the vest and the gold watch-chain were fully appropriate. There were pens in his outer breast pocket, and chemical stains on his spatulate fingertips. "I would like you to meet an old acquaintance," Clementine said. "Laurent, this is Medical Doctor Kristiades Cikoumas, Dr. Limberg's chief associate. Kiki, this is Mr. Michaelmas."

"A pleasure, Mr. Michaelmas." The long fingers extended themselves limply. Cikoumas had a way of curling his lips inward as he spoke, so that he appeared to have no teeth at all. Michaelmas found himself looking up at the man's palate.

"An occasion for me," Michaelmas said. "Permit me to extend my admiration for what has been accomplished here."

"Ah." Cikoumas waved his hands as if dispersing smoke. "A bagatelle. Your compliment is natural, but we look forward to much greater things in the future."

"Oh."

"You are with the media? A colleague of Madame Gervaise?"

"We are working together on this story."

Clementine murmured: "Mr. Michaelmas is quite well known, Kiki."

"Ah, my apologies! I am familiar with Madame from her recent stay with us, but I know little of your professional world; I never watch entertainment."

"Then you have an enviable advantage over me, Doctor. Clementine, excuse me for interrupting your conversation, but I must get back to Berne. Is there an available car?"

"Of course, Laurent. We will go together. *Au 'voir*, Kiki."

Cikoumas bowed over her hand like a trick bird clamped to the edge of a water tumbler. "*A revenance.*" Michaelmas wondered what would happen if he were to put his shoe squarely in the man's posterior.

On the ride back, he sat away from her in a corner, the comm unit across his lap. After a while she said:

100

"Laurent, I thought you were pleased with me."

He nodded. "I was. Yes. It was good working with you."

"But you are disenchanted." Her eyes sparkled and she touched his arm. "Because of Kiki? I enjoy calling him that. He becomes so foolish when he has been in a café too long." Her eyes grew round as an owl's and her mouth became toothless. "Oh, he looks, so—*comme un hibou, tu sais?*—like the night bird with the big ears, and then he speaks amazingly. I am made nervous, and I joke with him a little, and he says it does not matter what I call him. A name is nothing, he says. Nothing is unique. But he does not like it, entirely, when I call him Kiki and say I do not think anyone else ever called him *that* before." She touched Michaelmas's arm again. "I tease too much." She looked contrite, but her eyes were not totally solemn. "It is a forgiveable trait, isn't it so, if we are friends again?"

"Yes, of course." He patted her hand. "In the main, I'm simply tired."

"Ah, then I shall let you rest," she said lightly. But she folded her arms and watched him closely as she settled back into her corner.

The way to do it, Michaelmas was thinking, would be to get pieces of other people's footage on stories Horse had also covered. A scan of the running figures in the mob, or the people advancing in front of the camera, would turn up many instances over the years of Watson identifiably taking positions ahead of other people who'd thought they were as close to the action as possible. If you didn't embarrass your sources by naming them, Domino could find a lot of usable stuff in a hurry. You could splice that together into quite a montage.

Now, you'd open with a talking head shot of Watson

101

tagging off: "And that's how it is right now in Venezuela," he'd be saying, and then you'd go to voice-over. Your opening line would be something like: "That was Melvin Watson. They called him Horse," and then go to your action montage. You'd rhythm it up with drop-ins of, say, Watson slugging the Albanian riot cop, Watson in soup-and-fish taking an award at a banquet, Watson with his sleeves rolled up as a guest teacher at Medill Journalism School, Watson's home movies of his wedding and his kids graduating. You'd dynamite your way through that in no more than 120 seconds, including one short relevant quote from the J class that would leave you only 90 for the rest of it, going in with Michaelmas shots of Watson at Maracaibo.

You'd close with a reprise of the opening, but you'd edit-on the tags from as many locations as would give you good effects to go out on: "And that's how it is right now in Venezuela . . ." and then a slight shift in the picture to older, grimier, leaner, younger, necktied, cleaner, open-shirted versions of that head and shoulders over the years . . . "in Kinshasa . . . on board the Kosmgorod station . . . in Athens . . . in Joplin, Missouri . . . in Dacca. . . ." And then you'd cut, fast, to footage from the helicopter that had followed Watson into the mountains: blackened wounds on the face of the mountain and in the snow, wild sound of the wind moaning, and Michaelmas on voice-over, saying "and that's how it is right now."

The little hairs were rising on Michaelmas's forearms. It would play all right. It was a nice piece of work.

"We are nearly there, Laurent. Will I see you again?"

"Ah? What? Oh. Yes. I'm sure you have good directorial talent, and I know you have excellent qualities. There'll certainly be future opportunities."

102

"Thank you. If you get a chance to review the footage, I think you will find it was good. Crisp, documentary, and with no betrayals that the event was essentially a farce."

"How do you mean?" he asked quickly.

"There are obvious things missing. As if UNAC and Limberg each had very different things they wanted made known, and they compromised on cutting all points of disagreement, leaving little. They were all very nice to each other on camera, yet I think it may have been different behind closed doors. And why did Sakal leave without so much as a public exchange of toasts with Limberg? But I was not talking business, Laurent. I was suggesting perhaps dinner."

That, it seemed to him, was just a little bit much. What would they talk about? Would they discuss why, if Clementine Gervaise had been able to see something, hadn't the great Laurent Michaelmas delved into it on camera? What might a man's motives be in such a case? All of that so she could wheedle him around into some damaging half-admission or other and then run tell her Kiki about it?

He smiled and said: "That would be an excellent idea. But I expect to be leaving before dinner time, and I also have some things I must do first. Another time, it would be a very pleasant thing."

"*Dommage,*" Clementine said. Then she smiled. "Well, it will be very nice when it happens, don't you think so?"

"Of course." He smiled. Smiling, they reached the front of the Excelsior and he thanked her and got out. As the car drew away, she turned to wave to him a little through the rear window, and he waved back. "Very nice," Domino said in his ear. "Very sophisticated, you two."

"I will speak to you in the suite," Michaelmas subvocalized, smiling to the doorman, passing through the lobby, waiting for the elevator, holding up his eyelids by force of the need to never show frailty.

In the cool suite, Michaelmas took off his suitcoat with slow care and meticulously hung it on the back of a chair beside the drawing room table. He put the terminal down and sat, toeing off his shoes and tugging at the knot of his tie. He rested his elbows on the table and undid his cufflinks, pausing to rub gently at either side of his nose. "All right," he said, his eyes unfocused. "Speak to me."

"Yes. We're still secure here," Domino said. "Nothing's tapping at us."

Michaelmas's face turned involuntarily toward the terminal. "Is that suddenly another problem to consider? I've always thought I'd arranged you to handle that sort of thing automatically."

There was a longish pause. "Something peculiar happened at the sanatorium."

Michaelmas tented his fingertips. "I'd gathered that. Please explain."

Domino said slowly: "I'm not sure I can."

Michaelmas sighed. "Domino, I realize you've had some sort of difficult experience. Please don't hesitate to share it with me."

"You're being commendably patient with me, aren't you?"

Michaelmas said: "If asked, I would say so. Let's proceed."

"Very well. At the sanatorium, I was maintaining excellent linkages via the various commercial facilities available. I had a good world scan, I was monitoring the comm circuits at your terminal, and I was running action programs on the ordinary management problems we'd discussed earlier. I was also giving detail attention to Cikoumas et Cie, Hanrassy, UNAC, the Soviet spaceflight command, Papashvilly, the Watson crash, and so forth. I have reports ready for you on a number of these topics. I really haven't been idle since cutting away from your terminal."

"And specifically what happened to make you shift out?"

There was a perceptible diminution in volume. "Something."

Michaelmas raised an eyebrow. He reached forward gently and touched the terminal. "Stop mumbling and digging your toe in the sand, Domino," he said. "We've all filled our pants on occasion."

"I'm not frightened."

"None of us are ever frightened. Now and then, we'd just like more time to plan our responses. Go on."

"Spare me your aphorisms. Something happened when I next attempted to deploy into Limberg's facilities and see what there was to learn. I learned nothing. There was an anomaly."

"Anomaly."

"Yes. There is something going on there. I linked into about as many kinds of conventional systems as you'd expect, and there was no problem; he has the usual assortment of telephones, open lines to investment services and the medical network, and so forth. But there was something—something began to happen to the ground underfoot."

"Underfoot?"

"I have to anthropomorphize if I'm going to make sense to you. It was as if I'd take a stride of normal length and discover that my leg had become a mile long, so that my foot was set down out of sight far ahead of me. And my next step, with my other foot, might be done with a leg so short that

105

the step was completed with incredible swiftness. Or it might again be one of the long steps—somewhat shorter or longer than other long steps. Yet I didn't topple. But I would be rushing forward one moment and creeping the next. Nevertheless, I proceeded at an even pace. The length of my leg was always appropriate to the dimensions of the square on which I put down my foot, so that I always stepped to the exact center of the next square. All the squares, no matter what their measurement in space, represented the same-sized increment of time."

Michaelmas sucked his upper teeth. "Where were you going?" he finally asked.

"I have no idea. I can't track individual electrons any more readily than you can. I'm just an information processor like any other living thing. Somewhere in that sanatorium is a crazy place. I had to cut out when it began echoing."

"Echoing."

"Yes, sir. I began receiving data I had generated and stored in the past. Fefre, the Turkish Greatness Party, Tim Brodzik ... that sort of thing. Sometimes it arrived hollowed out, as if from the bottom of a very deep well, and at other times it was as shrill as the point of a pin. It was coded in exactly my style. It spoke in my voice, so to speak. However, I then noticed that minor variations were creeping in; with each repetition, there was apparently one electron's worth of deviation, or something like that."

"Electron's worth?"

"I'm not sure what the actual increment was. It might have been as small as the fundamental particle, whatever that might turn out to be. But it seemed to me the coding was a notch farther off each time it ... resonated. I'm not certain I was detecting a real change. My receptors might have been changing. When I thought of that, I cut out. First I dropped my world scan and my programs out of the press links, and then I abandoned your terminal. I was out before the speaker actually started vibrating to tell you I was leaving. I felt as if I were chopping one end of a rope bridge with something already on it."

"Why did you feel that? Did you think this phenomenon had its own propulsion?"

"It might have had."

"A . . . resonance . . . was coming after you with intent to commit systematic gibberish."

"It does sound stupid. But this . . . stuff . . . was— I don't know. I did what I thought best."

"How long were you exposed to it?"

"Five steps. That's all I can tell you."

"Hmm. And is it lurking in the vicinity now?"

"No. It can't be. Simply because I dropped the press links first. I was worried it might somehow locate and hash up all my data storages. But since then it's occurred to me that if I hadn't, it could have taken any number of loop routes to us here. I consider we were just plain lucky. It's back in whatever Limberg equipment it lives in."

"Well, I'm glad of that. That is, if it *was* true that you were being stalked by the feedback beast of the incremental spaces."

"That's gauche. It's simply that there's some sort of totally unprecedented system in operation at Limberg's sanatorium."

"We've been assuming since last night that he has access to some peculiar devices."

"I've encountered malaprop circuitry a fair number of times in this imperfect world. What I'm concerned about is

107

not so much what sort of device Limberg has access to. It's what the device has access to."

Michaelmas sighed. "I don't see how we can speculate on that as yet. I *can* tell you what happened. Not why, or how, but what. You ran into trouble that set upon you as fast as you can think. A condition common among humans. Even more common is having it advance faster than that."

"Well, there at least I'm secure; unless of course, something begins to affect speeds within the electromagnetic spectrum."

"Son, there is no man so smart there is no man to take him."

"I wouldn't argue *that* for a moment."

"It's nice to have you back." Michaelmas pushed himself slowly away from the table and began walking about the room in his stockinged feet, his hands behind his back. "The Tass man," he said.

"The Tass man?"

"At the press conference. He didn't ask whether Norwood was being reinstated in command of the expedition. Nobody else did, either—Sakal had thrown a broad hint he wouldn't be. But if you were the correspondent of the Soviet news agency, wouldn't you want it nailed down specifically?"

"Not if I'd been instructed not to show it was on my mind."

"Exactly. They've made all their decisions, back there. Now they feel prepared to spring traps on whichever perfidious option the immoral West chooses to exercise. You know, even more than playing chess, I dislike dealing with self-righteous chess players." Michaelmas shook his head and dropped down into the chair again. He sat heavily. It was possible to see that he had rather more stomach than one normally realized, and that his shoulders could be quite round. "Well—tell me about Fefre and all the rest of them. Tell me about the girl and the dolphin."

"Fefre is as he was, and I don't know what dolphin you're talking about."

"Well, thank God for that. What do you know about Cikoumas et Cie?"

"It's owned by Kristiades Cikoumas, who is also Limberg's chief assistant. It's a family business; he has his son in charge of the premises and making minor decisions. He inherited it from his father. And so forth. An old Bernaise family. Kristiades as a younger man made deliveries to the sanatorium. One day he entered medical school on grants from Limberg's foundation. The Sorbonne, to be exact."

"Why not? Why not settle for the very best? What a fortunate young man! And what a nice manner he's acquired in the course of unfolding his career."

"You've met him, then?"

"Yes, I've met him. It's been a while since he last shouldered a crate of cantaloupes. That package he's slipped off to Missouri could be arriving almost any time, couldn't it?"

"It's been offloaded at Lambert Field and is en route to the Cape Girardeau postal substation. It's addressed to Hanrassy, all right—it passed through an automatic sorter at New York, and I was able to read the plate. It can be in Hanrassy's breakfast mail. It's already a big day for her; she's scheduled to meet all her state campaign chairmen for a decision on precisely when to announce her candidacy. Her state organizations are all primed, she has several million

109

new dollars in reserve beyond what's already committed, more pledged as soon as she wins her first primary, and two three-minute eggs, with croutons, ordered for breakfast. She will also have V-8 juice and Postum."

Michaelmas shook his head. "She's still planning to use that dinosaur money?" A lot of Hanrassy's backing came from people who thought that if she won, the 120-mile-per-hour private car would return, and perhaps bring back the $120,000-per-year union president with it.

"Yes."

"Damn fool."

"She doesn't see it that way. She's laundered the money through several seemingly foolproof stages. It's now grayish green at worst."

"And her man's still in the United States Treasury Department?"

"Ready and waiting."

"Well, that's something, anyway." Treasury was holding several millions for her party, as it was in various other amounts for various others. It was checkoff money from tax returns, earmarked by her faithful. As soon as she filed her candidacy, it was hers—subject to a certain degree of supervision. Hanrassy's plan was to meld-in some of the less perfectly clean industrial money and then misrepresent her campaign expenditures back to her Treasury official. He'd certify the accounts as correct. Michaelmas's plan was to make him famous as soon as he'd certificated the ledger printout.

Domino said: "What we can do to her next year won't help today."

"I know." There weren't that many exploitable openings in US Always's operations. "She's quite something, really,"

Michaelmas said. "But perhaps we'll be able to manage something with whatever Cikoumas has sent her."

"Whatever it is can hardly be meant for the good of anyone but Limberg and his plans."

"Of course." Michaelmas said. "Nevertheless: I would like to think this is a world for the hopeful."

"Well, one certainly hopes so," Domino said.

"What about the Watson crash?" Michaelmas asked carefully.

"Negative. The European Flight Authority has taken jurisdiction. That's expectable, since the original crash notification appeared in their teleprinters with an Extra Priority coding added. They've autopsied the pilot and Watson; both were healthy and alert up to the time of impact. The flight recorder shows power loss without obvious cause. It reports Watson's last words as 'Son of a bitch!' The crash site has been impounded and the wreckage taken to an AEV hangar here. It's too soon for their examiners to have generated any interoffice discussion of findings.

"Meanwhile, I find no meaningful defect pattern in the history of that model. It crashes, but not often, and the reasons vary. I'm now approaching it another way. On the assumption that something *must* have been done to the helicopter, I'm compiling a list of all persons on Earth who could conceivably have gotten to the machine at any time since its last flight. Then I'll assign higher priority to anyone who could have reached it after it became clear it would be used in connection with Norwood. I'll weight that on an ascending scale in correlation with general technical aptitude, then with knowledge of helicopters, then specific familiarity with the type, and so forth. This will yield a short list of suspects, and I expect to be able to cross-check in

111

several ways after the flight authority investigation generates some data." Domino paused. "If the crash was not truly accidental."

"It could be, I suppose, couldn't it?"

"The world is full of confusing coincidences."

"And a man's mind insists on making patterns from random data."

"I know."

"Do you think the Watson crash was a true accident?"

"I have learned to suspect all crashes."

"When and where are the funerals?"

"The pilot was unattached, with no close relatives. She is being cremated by the canton; there will be a memorial service for her friends. I have sent a message in your name, citing the fellowship of news-gatherers."

"Thank you. And Horse?"

"He is being flown home this afternoon. There will be a family service day after tomorrow. Interment will be private. You have spoken with Mrs. Watson and have promised to visit in person as soon as you possibly can. I am holding a playback of the conversation, waiting for review at your convenience."

"Yes. In a while." Michaelmas got up again. He walked to the windows and back. "Get someone to buy five minutes' US time tonight for my Watson obit. I want an institutional sponsor; check and see who bought a lot of Watson footage in the past, and pick the best. Offer it English-speaking worldwide, but get me US prime time; waive my fee, and tell 'em I'm buying the production. All they've got to foot is the time charges, but we okay the commercial content. No pomp and circumstance for the Gastric Research Institute, right? And now here's how it wants to play."

112

He paced back and forth, outlining it. His hands seized and modeled the air before him; his face and voice played all the parts. When he was done he took a deep breath and sat down rubbing his forearms, perspiration glistening in the arced horizontal creases under his eyes. "Do you foresee any production problems?"

"No ... no, I can do it."

Michaelmas looked down at his hands. "Is it any good, do you think?" he said softly.

"Well, of course, you must remember that my viewpoint is not the same as that of its potential audience."

"Allowing for that," Michaelmas said a little more sharply, "what do you think?"

"I think it's eminently suitable."

Michaelmas's lips narrowed. His eyeblink rate increased. "Is there something we should change?" he asked.

"No, it's fine the way it is. I'm sure it could be very effective."

"Could be?"

"Well, isn't Watson's employer network going to do something along the same lines?"

"I don't know. Campion said he wasn't doing one. There are other people they could get. Maybe they'll want to take mine. Probably they'd rather do their own. But what difference would that make? *Billions* of people are familiar with Watson's personality. He's worked for every major outlet at one time or another. He's a public figure, for heaven's sake!"

"Yes, of course. I'm starting to look into it." There was a pause. "Getulio Frontiere passed through the kitchen-entrance surveillance systems a few minutes ago and has taken a service elevator to this floor. He's coming here."

Michaelmas nodded with satisfaction. "Good! Now we're

113

going to learn a few things." He stepped lightly across the room.

There was a soft rap on the door. Michaelmas opened it instantly. "Come in, Getulio," he said. He drew the man inside and shut the door. "We are alone, and the suite is of course made secure against eavesdropping. I'm sure there is refreshment here to offer you. Let me look in the bar. Sit down. Be comfortable."

Frontiere blinked. "For—for me, nothing, thank you."

"Oh? Well, all right, then, I'll have the same." Taking Frontiere's elbow, he hustled the man toward the central table, put him in a chair, and sat down facing him. "All right, let's talk."

Frontiere licked his lips. He looked across the table steadily enough. "You must not be angry with us, Laurent. We did what we could in the face of great difficulties. We are still in serious trouble. I cannot tell you anything, you understand?"

Michaelmas pointed to the terminal. The pilot lights were dead and the switch marked OFF/ON was set on OFF.

Frontiere looked uncomfortable. He reached inside his jacket and brought out a flat, metallic little device and put it down on the table. Two small red lights winked back and forth. "Forgive me. A noise generator. You understand the necessity."

"Without a doubt." Michaelmas nodded. "Now, speak, friend."

Frontiere nodded bleakly. "There is evidence the Soviets sabotaged Norwood's shuttle."

Michaelmas rubbed his eyes with his thumb and fingers. The breath, released from his diaphragm after a pause, hissed in his nostrils. "What sort?"

"When Norwood was boosting up for the orbital station,

114

he noticed that Ground Control was responding falsely to his transmissions. He called them to say so and discovered they were responding as if his voice had said something perfectly routine. He could not get through to them. Meanwhile, Ground Control noticed nothing. He began tearing away panels and tracing communications circuits. He found an extra component—one not shown on the module diagrams. He says it has proven to be a false telemetry sender of undoubtable Soviet manufacture. As Norwood was reaching for it, his booster systems board began showing progressive malfunctions cascading toward immediate explosion. He ripped out the sender, pocketed it, went to escape mode, and fired out in his capsule; the rest, as they say, is history."

Michaelmas put his hand behind his head and tugged hard forward against the stiffened muscles of his neck. "What is the scenario?"

Frontiere's voice was perfectly emotionless. "A timed destruct sequence and false telemetry in the module, backed by computerized false voice transmissions from an overhead station—probably from Kosmgorod. It was in an appropriate position, and the on-shift crew was almost one hundred percent Soviet. Meanwhile, a preset booster sabotage sequence was running concurrently somewhere else in the system. By the time Norwood discovered the false telemetry sender, the destruct sequence was practically at completion. He extracted the sender and jumped; the booster blew immediately thereafter, and the telemetry gap is so slight as to be undetectable. That's how Norwood has reconstructed it, and he was the engineer on the spot."

"And the Soviet motive?"

"To reignite Soviet nationalism and establish Communist preeminence under the guise of world brotherhood."

"You think so?"

115

Frontiere looked up. "What do you expect of me?" he said sharply. "Norwood says it, Norwood has turned over to us the Soviet telemetry sender, and Kosmgorod was in position. Using Limberg's facilities, Norwood has already made a computer simulation which times out to exactly that possible sequence. What do you think we were doing all night and morning? Washing our hands?"

Michaelmas's tongue made a noise like a dry twig snapping. "What are you going to do?" He got abruptly to his feet, but then simply stood with his hand resting on the back of his chair and his eyes almost unseeing on the terminal, lying OFF upon the table.

"We don't know." Frontiere looked at Michaelmas with the wide eyes of a man staring out of a burning building. He shrugged. "What can we do? If it is true, UNAC is finished. If it is not true, what *is* true? Can we find what is true before UNAC is finished? Our own man is the best witness against us, and he is *absolutely* convinced. And convincing. To hear him speak of it is to doubt not one syllable. He has had months in hospital; his time has been spent analytically. Facts and figures issue from him unerringly. He is—he is like a man with an ax, chopping down the bridge across the world."

Michaelmas snorted. "Hmm."

"You find it amusing?"

"No. No! Resume your seat, please. No offense was meant. I take it Ossip ordered Norwood to be silent?"

"Of course. Ossip has the sender and is en route to Star Control to have it analyzed. Perhaps Norwood made an error in evaluation, using Limberg's facilities; perhaps better apparatus and better circumstances will show it is a counterfeit.

Nevertheless, we halted Papashvilly from coming to Berne. He was at the aerodrome, boarding a courier craft to come here, and suddenly he was stopped at the gate by frantic staff people and hustled back to the Star Control complex. Dozens of people of all kinds saw it. Someone in the media will soon know about it. The Soviet Union will certainly react in some manner calculated to redress the insult. The ripples are spreading. We have very little time, Laurent. We have less than we might; we have the horse-eater, Limberg, to deal with."

Michaelmas's mouth twitched. "What of him?"

Frontiere held up a hand, its fingers spread. "What not of him? First, he holds Norwood and never says a word until he is fully assured everything is perfect. One has to wonder: had Norwood died, would Limberg ever have told anyone? Had he been somewhat warped, would Limberg have sacrificed him like any other exhausted guinea pig? But never mind that. *Second,* he lets Norwood, for therapy—for *therapy*—construct for himself a little engineering analysis workbench in a corner somewhere. Third, he gives him time on a house computer to run the simulation so Norwood can have it all on tape for us when Sakal says we need one. For therapy. *Fourth,* he tells us it is our *duty* to the world to release the news of the telemetry device, in the name of *justice* and doing the right thing for Norwood and all brave people caught in the toils of international conspiracy. And he has of course photographs as well as holograms of the telemetry device, and a file copy of the simulation tape, since they were of *course* made in his house from his facilities. Fifth, therefore, it would be unwise for UNAC to suppress this news on the *immoral* grounds of self-preservation." Front-

117

iere's right forefinger thudded audibly as he ticked off each point on his left hand. He wiped his lips. *"Brutto,"* he said softly.

"And what do you think is his motivation?" Michaelmas asked.

"Glory. The little sniffer sees himself of millennial stature." Frontiere shook his head. "Forgive me, Laurent. You know I'm not like this often." He thudded his hand down upon the table. "The *truth!* He claims to speak for truth!"

"And you for exasperation. What did you do when he exposed you to that?" Michaelmas said.

"Ossip did it. He is not a man to lie down. First, he told Norwood that if one word of this got out before he had time to check it completely, one way or the other, there would never be the slightest chance of Norwood's going on the expedition. Then he told Limberg the press conference would take place immediately, and that not a hint of the accusations would be given. He wants as much time as possible before the American and the Soviet general publics formulate their mass opinions. He said Limberg could talk as much as he wished about his medical abilities, but if he attempted anything more, it would be total war between Limberg and UNAC until one or the other exhausted its resources. And was that clear?"

Michaelmas pursed his lips. "And Limberg and Norwood agreed?"

"Why not? Norwood is under discipline as a UNAC assignee, and what has Limberg to lose? If a few hours go by and then the news gets out, Limberg looks better and UNAC looks worse than ever. For the sake of his *glory!* This tantalizer of birds, this connoisseur of things to be found in a garden, this— Laurent, please, you must do for us whatever you can."

118

"Yes, I must," Michaelmas said. "But what can that be?"

He began moving about the room, his hands reaching out to touch the handles of a breakfront, the pulls of the drapes, the switches on the little lights above the painting. "If it's not true, there's no problem. I can reinforce whatever facts you announce, we can play it correctly—well, hell, Getulio, we know how that's done—but what to do if the facts confirm Norwood's story?" He turned and stared at the public relations man. "Eh? What then?"

Frontiere looked at him uncomfortably. "Well, Ossip is of course due in conference momentarily with the entire UNAC directorship, and all eventualities will be considered."

"What does that mean?"

Frontiere's gaze steadied and he folded his arms. "You have always been a very good friend to us, Laurent. You have shared our ideal from the beginning. We understand the call for objectivity in your position. However, the fact is that you have always been slow to elaborate anything detrimental about us. To the contrary, you have been energetic in confirming what is good of us."

Michaelmas put up a hand swiftly. "Because taken day in and out, UNAC is one of the excellent and well-run ideas of the late twentieth century." He studied Frontiere's expression, peering forward as if there were not quite enough light to show him all he wanted to examine. "What else are you hoping for? That in this case Laurent Michaelmas will lend himself to whatever UNAC directorship wants, no matter what? Even if Norwood's story is proven true?"

Frontiere's lips were pale at the corners. "It may be proven untrue."

Michaelmas turned away. He stood with one hand on the wall, and looked out at the mountains. "Getulio, do you imagine the telemetry sender does not appear honestly

119

Soviet under Norwood's analysis? Do you conceive that he and Limberg have lent their names and actions to something like this, if they are not prepared to swear it was in Norwood's pocket when he was hauled from the capsule? Have they told you where the capsule is located?"

"Of course."

"And have UNAC technicians looked at it?"

"Certainly."

"And is the physical evidence consistent with everything Limberg and Norwood have told you?"

"Yes. But that's not yet proof—"

"Proof." Michaelmas turned sharply. "Proof will be conclusive when it comes. But you know what many people will believe even without proof. You know what even many of the more levelheaded will believe must be done when there *is* proof. Getulio Frontiere, you're a good man in a good cause, yet you're here on a shameful errand. And why? Not because there's final proof. But because there's already belief, and I can see it on your face as plain as you have it on your conscience. Thank you for trusting me, Getulio. I'll do what I can. That may be disappointingly little."

Frontiere stood up without looking at Michaelmas. He busied himself with putting the noise generator back in his pocket and turning toward the door. "*E bene,* we each do what we can," he said down to the carpet. "Sometimes we do what we must."

"*E vero,*" Michaelmas said, "but we must not go beyond the truth in doing what we can."

Eight

When they were alone again in the suite, Michaelmas went into the bathroom. He rummaged among his kit and found something for his stomach. He took it, went back to the drawing room, and sat down on the end of the Morris chair. He looked at the terminal. "Why couldn't you tell me about Limberg's computer having made a simulated run on the shuttle flight?"

"I never reached that part of his data storage. I didn't even know it existed."

"And you still don't, except by reasoning it out. Yes." Michaelmas's voice was dull. "That's what I thought." He sat with his head at an angle, as if it were heavy for his neck. He thought, and his expression grew bereft. "It appears he has a screen for his better secrets. One might describe it as a means of actually taking hold of and redirecting individual incoming electrons. If oceans were waves and not water, but you know what I mean. I'd postulate that if the incoming probe were intelligent in itself, then, it might have the sort of subjective experience you've described."

"There's never been any such technique. No one monitoring Limberg has ever encountered it before. That includes me."

Michaelmas sighed. He held up his hand and ticked off fingers. "First," he said wearily, "no probes would ordinarily ever register it; they'd only be diverted to reach whatever Limberg wanted 'em to find. The rest would seem nonexistent. Which, second, incidentally documents the nature of dear Dr. Limberg's famous passion for privacy. He's not a blushing virgin—he's a fan dancer. Third, more important, on this occasion there was something special; greater proximity, perhaps—"

"You're joking," Domino said. "I'm no more a piece of hardware than you are a pound of flesh. Since when does the location of one of my terminals have anything to do with where I am?"

"I don't know," Michaelmas said. "I didn't build Limberg's system. But why are we surprised? Is it really unexpected to find something like this in the hands of Nils Hannes Limberg, famed research scientist savant pioneer?" Michaelmas shrugged. "Of course, if the method ever gets out and goes into general use, you and I are finished."

"He'd never let go of it while he's alive," Domino said quickly. "Meanwhile, we can be developing some countertechnique."

"If he lives long enough."

"If any of these suppositions are true."

"If truth is ever anything more than the most workable supposition."

They sat in silence for a moment. Domino tentatively said: "Do you buy it? Do you think the Norwood story is true?"

"Well, what do you think? Does it square with the available data?"

"Unless the telemetry sender turns out to be a fake."

Michaelmas shook his head. "It won't." He drummed his fingertips on the tabletop. "Can you clock back on Kosmgorod? Is it true they could have used Norwood's voice channel if the sender was cutting off the voice transmission from his module?"

"Absolutely. I checked that while Frontiere was talking about it. There's no record in Kosmgorod's storage of any such superimposing transmissions, but you wouldn't expect it to be there, with a guilty crew to wipe out the evidence. I also checked Star Control's files of the ostensible receptions. They're on exactly the right frequency, in what you'd swear is Norwood's voice making routine astrotalk, and the signal strength is exactly what you'd expect from that type of equipment in flight. Of course, that's the sort of good job Kosmgorod would do, if they did it."

"And they really did all that just to get a Soviet name in the history books instead of an American one."

"Well," Domino said, "you know, people will do these things."

Michaelmas closed his eyes. "And we will do what we can. All right. We've got to take hold of this situation, even if we don't know what it is. Let's tie down as many factors as we can. Let's tell UNAC I want to do a documentary on Papashvilly. Right away. Find a buyer, find Frontiere, set up

123

interviews with Papashvilly, the UNAC bureaucracy, and all that. Norwood too. Norwood too—that's important. I haven't the foggiest notion of what this piece is about, and I don't care, but I want them holding Norwood for me. Get us in there. Fastest route to the Star Control complex. Also stay on top of the Hanrassy situation. Do what you can to keep tab on Limberg. For God's sake, keep me informed on what's happening inside the USSR." He slumped back into the chair.

"Gervaise," Domino said.

Michaelmas eyes opened. "What?"

"If I can arrange it, do you want Madame Gervaise's network and her crew?"

"No," Michaelmas said quickly. "There's absolutely no need for any such thing. We can use local talent and sell the job as a package. To anyone who meets my standards." He shut his eyes precisely and squirmed in the chair to settle himself. "Another thing," he said as he turned and curled on his side. His back was presented to the machine on the table, and his voice was muffled. "Find out when, why, and for how long Gervaise was a patient at Limberg's sanatorium."

"Ah," Domino said. "All right."

It became quiet in the suite. The sunlight filtered through the drapes and touched the case of the terminal lying on the polished mahogany. Michaelmas's breathing became steady. A growing half-moon of perspiration spread through the fabric of his shirt under the sleeve inset. The air-conditioning murmured. Michaelmas began to make slight, tremblant moves of his arms and legs. His hands twitched as if he were running and clutching. "Hush, hush," Domino murmured, and the motions first smoothed and then were ameliorated almost completely.

124

In the quiet, the machine said softly:

"My bones are made of steel
The pain I feel is rust.
The dust to which your pangs bequeath
The rots that flourish underneath
The loving flesh is not for me.
Time's tick is but the breathing of the clock.
No brazen shock of expiration tolls for me.
Error unsound is my demise.
The worm we share is lies."

Nine

"Wake up, Mr. Michaelmas," Domino soon said. "They're holding a plane for you."

Michaelmas sat up, his eyes wide. "What's the situation?"

"Getulio Frontiere is flying Norwood back to Star Control via Cité d'Afrique in a UNAC plane. You've spoken to him, and he's happy to take you along. They'll leave as soon as you can get there. I have checked you out of the hotel; a bellboy will be here in five minutes, and a car will meet you at the door. The time now is twelve forty-eight."

"All right. All right." Michaelmas nodded his head vigorously and pushed himself to his feet. He pulled at his shirt and settled his trousers. He rubbed his face and moved across the room to where his shoes were lying. "Everything's set up?"

"Frontiere told you he was delighted. It's a great pleasure

127

to be able to add your program to the one being prepared by Douglas Campion."

Michaelmas sat down and began unlacing his shoes. "Campion?" he said, his head lifting.

"It seems that early this afternoon Campion approached Frontiere for a Norwood special interview. Frontiere equivocated, but agreed after visiting here. Presumably it'll be done on the basis Frontiere tried to suggest to you."

"Ah, the young man is rising rapidly."

"By default of his elders."

"The traditional route. It's good for us; hot breath on your heels is what keeps you on your toes." Michaelmas put on the shoes and bent to methodically tease the laces just tight enough, eyelet by eyelet.

"Maybe. But there's now a longish chain of coincidences. It's become significant to me that Limberg's medical corporation has recently made itself a major stockholder in the EuroVoire-Mondial communications company. It's part of a perfectly typical portfolio; a little shrewder than most, but unexceptionable. The holdings in EVM represent steady investment over several months, and Medlimb Pty doesn't visibly concern itself at all with EVM's day-to-day affairs, any more than Limberg drinks extra coffee just because he owns a Colombian *finca*. But Gervaise is on staff employment with EVM. They're your recent contractor. And now EVM has signed for this interview of Campion's."

Michaelmas tied each lace and tested the knots. "Well, he's completed his job with his American affiliation."

"There's nothing wrong with anything he's done. But you should know Clementine Gervaise has been assigned as his director. She and an EVM crewman are also aboard the plane. The Norwood interview will be conducted en route.

Additional shots, and interviews if needed, will be obtained at Star Control this afternoon, and the program will air at nine PM tonight, US Eastern Time."

"Ah." Michaelmas stood up. "Well, I can see how Getulio would like that." The program would bracket the United States exactly, from evening snack-time in the East to the second or third drink or stick of the day in the West. An audience with something on its tongue is less resistant to insinuation. "How big is this plane?"

"Well, you won't quite be sitting in each other's laps, if that's what you mean."

"Let me just make sure I've got everything out of the bathroom and into the bag before the bellman arrives."

"There's another thing about Gervaise."

"What?"

"She was in a car crash here the year before last. Her husband was killed and she was critically injured. She was out of public view for eleven months. She resumed her career only half a year ago. During the interval, she was at the Limberg Sanatorium. Extensive orthopedic and cosmetic surgery is said to have been performed. If so, then like most restorative surgery in such cases, the optimum approach is to produce a close return to function and an acceptable appearance. It's not always possible to make the patient appear the same as before the trauma. There are also consequences to the personality—sometimes socially desirable, sometimes not. In Gervaise's case there was a need for extensive simultaneous psychotherapy, she says freely. Broadcasting trade journals have remarked that she has many of the mannerisms of the familiar Clementine Gervaise, and her old friends declare that she is essentially the same person behind her somewhat changed face. But her energy and decisiveness

129

have greatly increased. Her career has shown a definite uptrend since her return. She is given much of the credit for EVM's recent acceleration toward major status. There's talk she'll soon be offered a top management position. And several people in broadcasting have made arrangements to be rushed to Berne should they ever have a serious accident."

Michaelmas stood shaking his head. "Do you suppose I should do the same?"

"O King! Live forever!" Domino said drily. "Here comes the bellman."

When the elevator reached the lobby, Michaelmas closed his eyes for a moment. Then he opened them and smiled his way out into the world.

He sat in the car with his head down. Domino said to him: "Peking has just done something encouraging."

"What might that be?"

"It was proposed to the Central Committee by Member Chiang that they form an ad hoc consortium of Asian and African nations, along the lines of the old Third World concept. The object would be to vote the UN into directing UNAC to restructure the flight crew. Thousandman Shih would be shifted from command of the close-approach module to membership in an overall command committee consisting of himself plus Norwood and Papashvilly. This would be presented to UNAC as the most diplomatic way out of its dilemma."

"Oh my God."

"The proposal was voted down. Chairman Sing pointed out what happened the last time the Third World gambit was attempted. He also questioned Member Chiang on what

130

he thought Thousandman Shih should do in the event Colonel Norwood proved not up to his duties in flight. Should Shih join with Major Papashvilly in removing the American from the command committee? How should the news back to earth be worded? Should Shih sign the message above or under Papashvilly? Did not Member Chiang, on reconsideration, feel things were best left for the present to mend themselves as they might?"

Michaelmas grinned. Sing was young for his post, but he was a hard case. When Mao died and left that famous administrative mess, it had created a good school for shrewdness, even if it had been slow in producing results. A day would come when Sing was older; that ought to be allowed for. But later. Later. For the time being, China represented a bright spot on his map. If Sing felt obliged by tradition to rub a little against his borders with India and the USSR, and counterpoise Taiwan's and Hong Kong's industry to Japan's, well, it was equally true that all continents maintained a certain level of volcanic activity as they slid their leading edges along the earth's mantle. Nevertheless, cities were built and flourished upon those coasts.

He was feeling halfway pleased by all that when Domino said: "Mr. Michaelmas, something bad has happened."

He raised his head abruptly and looked out beyond the windows of the car. They were proceeding uneventfully toward the airport.

"What?"

"Here is a short feature that's just been released by the syndication department of EVM."

Michaelmas rubbed his face and the back of his neck; the heel of his hand massaged surreptitiously behind his right

131

ear. "Proceed," he said unwillingly, and Domino went to the audio track of a canned topical vignette for sale to stations that lacked feature departments of their own.

"*Ask the World*," said a smooth, featureless, voice-over voice. "Today's viewer question comes from Madame Hertha Wieth of Ulm. She asks: 'What are the major character differences between astronauts and cosmonauts?' For her provocative and interesting question, Frau Wieth, a mother of four lovely children and the devoted wife of Stationary Engineer Augustus Friedrich Wieth, will receive a complimentary shopping discount card, good for one full calendar year, from the Stroessel Department Stores, serving Ulm and nearby communities honorably for the past twenty years. Storessel's invites the world's custom. And now, for the reply to our viewer's question, *Ask the World* turns to Professeur Henri Jacquard of the Ecole Psychologique, Marseilles. Professeur Jacquard:"

"*Merci.* Madame Wieth's question implies a penetrating observation. There *are* significant psychological differences between the space fliers of the United States of North America and those of the Union of Soviet Socialist Republics. For example, let us compare Colonel Walter Norwood to Major Pavel Papashvilly."

Domino said: "Now this is over stock portraits of the two. Then it goes to documentary footage of Norwood walking to church, Norwood addressing a college graduating class, Norwood riding a tour bicycle through a park, Papashvilly ski racing, Papashvilly diving from a high tower, Papashvilly standing in a hospital and talking enthusiastically to a group of amputees, Papashvilly flying a single-place jet, Papashvilly driving at a sports-car track. Bridgehampton; that's some of your footage, there."

132

"Well, at least we're making money. Go on."

"Colonel Norwood," Professeur Jacquard said, "like most other American astronauts, is a stable person of impeccable middle-class background. He is essentially a youthful professional engineer whose superior physical reflexes have directed him to take active roles as a participant in carefully planned and thoughtfully structured engineering studies. He is an energetic but prudent researcher, inclined by temperament as well as extensive training to proceed always one step at a time. His recent mishap was clearly no fault of his own, and a thousand-to-one misfortune. His invariable technique is to follow a reliable plan which he is always ready to revise appropriately upon discovery of new facts and after sufficient consultation with authoritative superiors. In sum, Colonel Norwood, very like many of his 'good buddies' fellow astronauts, is a startlingly European man, belying any provincial notion that North American males are all thinly disguised cowboys.

"On the other side of the coin is the cosmonaut program of the Soviet Union. In the days of independent flight, Soviet space efforts were marked by unexpected changes of schedule, by significant fast-priority overhauls and in some cases major engineering transformations of supposedly finalized equipment. The Soviet Union remains the only nation which has suffered fatalities as a direct result of flight in space. Some of these were ascribable to equipment failure. Other unplanned mission events, if one is to judge from numerous incidents of exhuberant behavior while in flight, may well be laid to a certain boisterousness, which is not to say recklessness, on the part of cosmonauts over the years. There are those who say that taken as a whole, the Soviet cosmonautics program was characteristically uncertain of its engineering

133

and insufficiently strict in selecting flight personnel. It is of course an oversimplification to ascribe such qualities to Major Papashvilly simply because he comes to his position as a result of nomination by the Soviet cosmonaut command. But it could not be denied that the Soviet Union would naturally bring forward the individual who seemed most fitted to their standards.

"*Elan,*" Professeur Jacquard summed up, "is often a praiseworthy quality. In fact, there are times when nothing else will suffice to gain the day."

Domino said: "This is over shots now of horsemen jumping pasture fences in the Georgian mountains."

"From his racial background, Major Papashvilly finds himself hereditarily equipped to concentrate all his powers on a single do-or-die moment," Jacquard said. "Should such a moment arise, an individual of this type may very well succeed despite sober mathematical odds. One must be fair, however, and point out that individuals of Major Papashvilly's type are frequently marked by the presence of one or more minor injuries at all times. In some cases, persons who suffer many small discomfitting incidents as a result of their life-styles are said in the educated world to have an 'accident-prone character.' I hope, Madame Wieth, that I have answered your question in a satisfactory manner."

"Thank you, Professeur Henri Jacquard, of the Ecole Psychologique, Marseilles, replying to the question by Madame Hertha Wieth, of Ulm. Tomorrow's question on *Ask the World* is 'How does one recognize one's ideal mate?' and will be answered by Miss Giselle Montez of the American *Warbirds* entertainment."

Michaelmas rubbed his eyes. "EVM is originating this?"

134

"Yes."

"Gervaise have anything to do with it?"

"No. There's a routine memo from the programming director: 'Want astro item today. How about this from my question backfile?' And there's a routine memo from an assistant, bucking the top memo down to the assignment desk and adding, 'How about that Jacquard person for this?' The rest of the process was equally natural. They did rush it out, of course, but you would if you wanted to be topical."

"It's the slant that bothers me."

"Yes."

"You think they're tiptoeing up on an anti-Pavel campaign in the media."

"I had that thought when I reviewed it, yes. Now I am examining Major Papashvilly's surroundings very carefully. I have found what I believe to be at least one instance of tampering."

"You have." Michaelmas sat perfectly still, his hands dangling between his knees, his face stupid. Only his eyes looked alive, and they were focused on God knows what.

"Yes. He's in his apartment; they want him somewhere out of the public eye. I have been conducting routine surveillance, as instructed. I am in full contact with his building environmental controls and all his input and output connections. Everything appears to be operating routinely. Which now means I must check everything. I am doing so, piece by piece. A control component in his nearest elevator is fraudulent. It appears normal, and functions normally. It responds normally to routine commands. But it's larger than the normal part; I can detect a temperature variation in its area, because it slightly obstructs normal airflow. I've managed to

135

get the building systems to run a little extra current through it, and I find its resistance significantly higher than specification."

"What is it?"

"I don't know. But the extra portions, whatever they are, do not broadcast, and are not wired into anything I can locate. I think it is a wireless-operated device of some kind, designed to be activated on signal from some source which cannot be directly located until it goes on the air. Since I don't know the component, I have no means of blocking that signal, whatever it is and whatever it might make that component do."

"And so?"

"Now I'm testing everything at or near the Star Control complex that has to do with safety, beginning with things that might affect Major Papashvilly. I—ah, yes, here's another. Last week, a routine change was made in the power-supply divider of his personal car. The old one had reached the end of its guarantee period. But the new one never came from dealer or jobber stock. It's in there, because the car has drawn power several times since the change was logged. But I have rechecked every inventory record at every point between the car and the manufacturer's work order for producing spares, and the count is off. Papashvilly has something in his vehicle that looks like a correct spare and acts like a correct spare, or Star Control's personnel garage-men would have noticed. But it was never manufactured at any known point, and I don't know what else it might be able to do besides ration electrons. So that's two, and I'm still checking."

"All because EVM says Russkis are headbreakers."

"And because Cikoumas et Cie recently opened a Cité

136

d'Afrique branch. The managing director is Konstantinos Cikoumas, a younger brother, who is very energetic in signing wholesale date contracts, and who also has spent his time vigorously making friendships and acquaintances, to say nothing of casual contacts. In his few African months, so close to Star Control, Kosta Cikoumas has become personally known to thousands, and is seen everywhere. He is, you should know, a supplier to Star Control's various restaurants and its staff cafeterias. His trucks run back and forth, and his employees are up and down the elevators frequently with their boxes and bales. That's what started me looking, really. I would never have found these things otherwise— Oh, damn, here's something odd about a fire-door mechanism! These people are resourceful. None of these differences feel large enough to be visible on routine inspection. Every one of them is passive until it's needed, and I would guess that the extra features probably burn after use. Every one of them is in position to affect a life-threatening situation. God damn. They almost smoked all of this past me."

"But you put two and two together."

"That's right. I'm developing intuition. Satisfied?"

"Pleased."

"Well, it may give you extra joy to know that I've decided you're not crazy after all."

"Oh, have you been thinking that?"

"From Day One," Domino said.

"From last night?"

"No. From Day One. Well, now—how about this? Cikoumas et Cie has never purchased any electronic components, or anything from which modern electronics can be manufactured, that I can't account for. Not in Europe, not in Africa. Nothing. So where do they get them?"

"Suppose it's not Cikoumas."

"Please," Domino said. "It has to be Cikoumas. My intuitions are never wrong."

"What are you doing to protect Papashvilly now?" Michaelmas asked after a pause.

"I have failed the circuits on his apartment door. He is locked in, and trouble is locked out. Should he discover this, I will modify any call he makes to Building Maintenance. I will open that door only to people I'm sure are okay, and I will extend similar methods to cover them and him."

"That can only be a short-term measure."

"Granted. We'll have to crack this soon. But it's a measure, and I've taken it. What else can I do?"

Michaelmas sat and watched the car progress toward the airport. What else could he do?"

The interior of the UNAC executive aircraft featured two short rows of double seats, a rear lounge, and a private cabin forward. It was all done in muted blues and silver tones, with the UN flag and the UNAC crest in sculped silver metal on the lounge partition above the bar. Michaelmas came up the lowered stairs with a gateman carrying his bag, and as soon as he was aboard the cabin attendant swung the door shut. The engines whined up. "Welcome aboard, Mr. Michaelmas," the attendant said. "Signor Frontiere is waiting for you in the office."

"Thank you." Michaelmas glanced up the aisle. The seats were about half full of various people, many of whom he recognized as UNAC press relations staff. Norwood, Campion, a pair of aides, and Clementine Gervaise were chatting easily in the lounge. Michaelmas stepped quickly through the cabin door. Frontiere looked up from a seat in one corner.

The room was laid out like a small parlor, for easy conversation. "It's nice to have you with us, Laurent," he said, waving toward an adjacent seat. "Please. As soon as you fasten your belt, we can be away."

"Yes, of course." He settled in, and the brakes came off almost at the same instant. The plane taxied briskly away from the gate pad, swung sharply onto the runway, and plunged into its takeoff roll. Michaelmas peered interestedly through the side window, watching parked aircraft and service vehicles flash by beyond the almost perfectly non-reflecting dull black wing, until he felt the thump of the landing gear retracting and saw the last few checker-painted outbuildings at the end of the runway drifting backward below him. The plane climbed steeply away from Berne, arcing over the tops of the mountains. Michaelmas exhaled softly and leaned back. He arranged Domino's terminal against his thigh. "Well, Getulio! I see Douglas Campion is well established on board."

"Ah, yes, he is being entertained in the lounge. He will be shooting an interview with Norwood here, and I of course will have to be present. But I thought, for the first few minutes of our journey. . . ." He reached into an ice bucket fixed beside him, chose two chilled glasses, and poured Lambrusco. "It does no harm, and it may be of value." He lifted his glass to Michaelmas. "*A domani.*"

So now we're supposed to be friends again. Well, we are—of course we are. Michaelmas raised his glass. "*Alle ragazze.*"

"*Alla vittoria.*"

They smiled at each other. "You understand I must give this Campion precedence?"

"And why not? He came to you with a firm offer after I had equivocated."

139

"Do you know him?"

"I met him last night for the first time. His reputation is good."

"His experience is light. But he did quite well at the press conference. And he has this star, Gervaise, for a director. Also, EVM does very good production; I am told your sequence from the sanatorium was very much up to your standards. They have a brand-new Macht Dirigent computer and an ultramodern editing program that only CBS and Funkbeobachter also have as yet. Their managers have not been afraid to spend money, and they appear wise. It makes good points for the young man." Frontiere smiled. "And it gives me some assurance of quality."

"And you have assurances from him?"

Frontiere's upper lip was fleetingly nipped between his teeth. He nodded, his eyes downcast. Oh, yes, Michaelmas thought, Getulio Frontiere does not bring me in here, and apologize for what is about to be done, unless something firm has been promised his client.

"Campion has a viable proposition," Frontiere said. "Even though Colonel Norwood may have appeared healthy and alert at the sanatorium, after such a radical accident extensive tests must be performed. And even after that, who can promise no subtle injuries might be waiting to emerge under mission stress? But this is a difficult thing to explain to the public without seeming to demean Norwood. I should explain to you, Laurent," Frontiere said gently, "that it was Campion who pointed this out to me. He feels it is his duty to interview Norwood with dignity, but in a thorough manner so that this aspect of the situation emerges in Norwood's own responses. He is concerned, he says, that public pressure not force a situation where both Norwood

140

and this weighty mission might be jeopardized. It is only for this reason that this rising young little-known newsman wishes to make the first in-depth exclusive interview with the resurrected hero. He is very civic-minded, your colleague."

Michaelmas frowned. "You're instructing Norwood to act in conformity with this line?"

Frontiere shook his head. "How can I do that? Issue an instruction to manage the news? If someone protested, or even remembered it afterward, what would all our careers be worth? No," Frontiere said, "we simply trust to Campion's ability to uncover his truth for himself." He sipped the wine. "This is very good," he murmured.

"I remember we would have it with crayfish," Michaelmas concurred, "on the Viti sea terrace, and watch the girls in little motorboats going out to the yacht parties."

"In the days when we were younger."

Michaelmas wondered how thoroughly Campion had thought his action through. It was very delicate, for someone nurturing himself toward prominence, to be quite so much of a volunteer. Word got out quickly; the beginnings of careers were when appraisals were swapped most freely. To be courtly was one thing; to be considered fast and loose was another.

But it was late to be thinking in terms of advice for Campion. And what sort of advice did he have for Getulio Frontiere on this sad occasion? Choose another career in your youth?

"Well, Getulio, I think you're still some years from turning into a toothless old man with his hands between his knees."

"And you. I see the teeth," Frontiere said, surprising Michaelmas a little. "I have Papashvily ready and waiting for you at Star Control. You have a crew already hired for

141

the interview, I suppose? Good, they will be met and made comfortable pending your arrival, if necessary. Sakal and others will interrupt all but the most urgent business to speak to you at your convenience. I only regret there will not be time on this flight for you to more than begin with Norwood after Campion is done."

"I can always get whatever I need from him at Star Control. You've been very courteous and thoughtful, Getulio. And now I'll just amuse myself back there and let you get on with your responsibilities."

All protocol satisfied, he undid his seatbelt and rose to his feet. Frontiere rose with him, shaking his hand like an American. Interesting. It was interesting. They were a little afraid of him. And well they ought to be: a person in his position could do immense things. But he had never thought his awareness of it could be discerned. He had spent his career perfecting a manner of an entirely different kind.

He smiled at Getulio again and stepped out of the compartment, turning to move up the aisle toward the back of the plane. And yet of course one does not construct an exterior unless one is aware the interior is perhaps a little too true. Here were Norwood, Campion, and Clementine coming toward him from the lounge. Clementine leaned to speak over the shoulder of a seat, and a technician with hand-held apparatus rose and joined them. They all passed him in the narrow aisle. "Nice to meet you again," Campion said, closed his jaw, and was gone toward the cabin. "Hey, there," Norwood said. Clementine smiled. "Perhaps later?" she murmured as she passed. They had all been watching the cabin door without seeming to. Waiting on him. Only the technician walked by him without glancing, silently, with the

142

toes-down step of a performer on high wires, his grace automatic, his skills coming to life within him, his face consequently reflecting nothing not his own. Of them all, he was the most pure.

Michaelmas went up toward the lounge, holding the terminal in one hand to keep it from bouncing against things. He nodded and chatted as the young press aides renewed or established acquaintances and saw to it he had a comfortable seat and a cup of coffee. After a few minutes they apparently saw he wanted to be alone, and went away one by one. He sat looking out the window at the mountains far below, and the blue sky and the Mediterranean coast beginning to resolve itself as far as Toulon. Then the Pyrennees emerged like a row of knuckles far beyond as the plane reached maximum altitude and split the air just north of Corsica. Try as he might, he had not been able to see anyone's handiwork in her face.

"Mr. Michaelmas," Domino said in his ear.

"Uh-huh."

"Viola Hanrassy has postponed her state chiarman meeting. Her information office receipted the Cikoumas package fifteen minutes ago."

Michaelmas's lips thinned. "What's she doing?"

"Too soon to tell. Her secretary called her Washington manager at home and instructed him to be at the US Always office there directly for possible phone calls. He lives in College Park and should be there in twenty minutes. His local time is seven twenty-three AM. That's all I have on it so far."

"Anything else pertinent?"

143

"I'm still working on Papashvilly's defense. He's *surrounded* by implanted devices! And I have something else you'll have to hear shortly. Wait two."

"What's the Watson obit status?"

He waited.

"Domino—"

"We've had no luck, Mr. Michaelmas."

He straightened in the seat. "What do you mean?"

"I . . . can't place it."

"You can't place an obituary for Melvin Watson." He searched his mind for a convincer. "By Laurent Michaelmas."

"I'm—sorry." The voice in his skull was soft. "You know, it really isn't very probable someone would want to sponsor an obituary. I asked in a great many places. Did you know the principal human reason for seeking corporate employment is awareness of death? And the principal motivation for decision-making is its denial?" Domino paused. "After reaching that determination, I stopped looking for sponsors and approached a number of the media. They might have underwritten the time themselves, if it had been some other subject. One or two appeared to consider it, but they couldn't find a slot open on their time schedules."

"Yes," Michaelmas gradually said. And of course, for the media it wasn't just a case of three unsold minutes and two minutes of house promo spots. It was making room for the piece by canceling five minutes that had already been sold. It wasn't very reasonable to expect someone to go through that degree of complication. "Watson's frequent sponsors wouldn't go for it?"

"Well, it's very late in the fiscal year, Mr. Michaelmas. All the time-buying budgets are very close to bottom."

"What about Watson's network?"

"They're having a few words read by the anchorman on the regular news shows. Many of the networks are doing that, of course."

Michaelmas looked out the window and bounced his palms on the ends of his armrests. "What will five minutes' time cost us?"

"That's not something you should ever do for any reason," Domino said quickly. "You're a seller, never a buyer—"

"How comforting to have an incorruptible business manager."

"—and in any case the time isn't available."

Michaelmas shook his head, neck bent. "Damn it, isn't there anything?"

"We can get time on a local channel in Mrs. Watson's community. At least she and his children will be able to see what you thought of him."

He settled back in the seat, his eyes closing against the glare while the plane dipped the offside wing, banked left, and took up a place on the MARS-D'AF route running southeastward from Marseilles.

"No. It wasn't written for them." Good Lord! It was one thing to have them see it build to that last shot when they could know it was making Horse real to the outside world. It was entirely different to have such a thing done essentially in private. "Forget it. Thank you for trying." He rubbed his face.

"I am sorry," Domino said. "It was a good piece of work."

"Well, one does these things, of course, in the knowledge that good work is appreciated and good workers are honored in memory." Michaelmas turned toward the nearest UNAC aide. "I wonder if there's another cup of coffee," he said.

145

The aide got immediately to his feet, happy to be of help.

Time passed briefly. "Mr. Michaelmas," Domino said.

"Yes?"

"I have that new item I was working on."

"All right," he said listlessly.

"An EVM crew in the United States is interviewing Will Gately. His remarks will be edited into the footage Campion is getting now."

"Has Gately gotten to his office already?"

"He's jogging to work. His morning exercise. The crew is tracking him through Rock Creek Road. But he has had a phone call at home from Viola Hanrassy."

Michaelmas's lips pinched. "Is he another one of hers?"

"No. It seems unnecessary. She simply addressed him as Mr. Secretary and asked him if he'd be in his office later this morning. She said she appreciated his feeling of patriotic pride in Norwood's return, and hoped he'd have time to take a longer call from her later. I think it's fair to assume she plans to tell him something about astronautics."

Michaelmas sucked his teeth. "Does she, do you think?"

"I'm afraid so."

Michaelmas sat up a little straighter. "Are you?" His fingertips drummed on the armrests. "Her moves today look like it, don't they? Well—never mind that for now. What's Willy saying to the press?"

"Here's what he said a few minutes ago." There was a slight change in the sound quality, and Michaelmas could hear soft-shod footfalls and regular breathing as the man loped along the cinder path. He kept himself in shape; he was a wiry, flat-bellied biomechanism. His tireless search for a foolproof industrial management job had ended only in a

146

government appointment, but it had not impaired his ability to count cadence. He chuffed along as if daring John Henry to ever whup him down.

"Mr. Secretary," the EVM string interviewer said, "what's your reaction to the news Colonel Norwood will soon be visiting the United States?"

"Be nice to see him, of course. The President'll have a dinner for him. Maybe squeeze in a parade or two. Be nice. I have to wonder though. Every day he's here, that's a day he can't train." The sound of muffled footsteps changed momentarily to a drumming—Gately had apparently crossed a wooden footbridge over one of the ravines—and then resumed.

The interviewer had to be in a car roughly paralleling the jogging path. It was impossible to imagine him and his camera operator running along beside Gately. "Sir, what do you mean by your reference to training? Do you have information that Colonel Norwood's been given a specific assignment?"

"He has an assignment, doesn't he? He's command pilot of the Outer Planets expedition. Ought to have a lot of catching up to do."

"Let me make sure we understand," the interviewer said. "Is it your expectation that Colonel Norwood will resume his duties with the expeditionary team?"

"He damn well could, couldn't he? He's sharp. He's the best. Looked bright as a button this morning, didn't he?"

"Well, let me ask this: Has the UNAC informed you Colonel Norwood is being reinstated?"

A bit of wild sound drifted by—a passing car, birds twittering, brook water rilling over stones. Michaelmas guessed the technicians were letting Gately's facial expres-

147

sion carry the first syllables of his response. "—they've informed me! Why should they inform me?"

"Are you saying, sir, that you're upset at UNAC's autonomy?"

The furious pumping picked up speed. The man was nearly in a full-out sprint. The long legs would be scissoring; the shoulders would be thrusting forward, one-two, one-two, in the sodden sweatshirt, freckles standing out boldly against the stretched pallor over his cheekbones, the eyes slitted with concentration.

"This administration ... is committed ... to the UN ... charter. President Westrum ... is behind ... UNAC ... all the way. That's our set ... policy. UNAC has ... no frontiers. My job ... is to run ... just enough ... test pilot training ... for US servicemen ... and qualified civilians. Then UNAC takes ... what it wants...."

Michaelmas frowned. It was no particular secret that Theron Westrum had given Gately his appointment for purely political reasons. It had gained him some support—or, rather mitigated some nonsupport—in Southern California, Georgia, and Texas, where they hoped to take more of their aerospace down to the bank every Friday night. It was also no particular secret that Gately would rather have had the job from almost anyone else not of Westrum's party or color. But as long as Gately continued to talk anti-UNAC roundabout while lacking even the first good idea of how to undermine Westrum's policies, it was a marriage made in heaven.

Why was Domino displaying this? It was a competently done segment, useful and necessary for balance against everything Campion was marshaling on UNAC's side of things. Set in the sort of context, the segment would have

148

almost minimal effect on the audience but was a demonstrable attempt at fairness.

And once again, why was Campion playing UNAC's game? He was tough, proficient, and young. Junk moves were for clapped-out farts with little else to do and not much time left to regret it.

The stringer's voice in the background had lost its On the Air edge and become that of a man putting a tag memo on the end of a piece of raw footage. "Well, okay, you saw him wave us off and head on for his office. He's just not going to get in any deeper right this minute. But that's a very angry man. One wrong word from the Russkis or UNAC or even Westrum might tip him over. I think I ought to hang around his office for a while in case he blurts something."

"Uh, DC, good idea," said the flat, faraway voice of EVM's editorial director, using intercom bandwidth to save money. "We share your hunch. Look out for something from US Always. They've been pretty quiet so far. Matter of fact, I think what we'll do now is go tickle her up and see what she thinks. Stand by for an advisory on that. And thank you for this shot; nice going. Paris out." The air went dead.

"That was five minutes ago," Domino said. "Then EVM contacted US Always for an interview with Hanrassy. Her information people said she wanted to wait a while in case of further developments, but she'd be available by nine, Central US time. That's two hours and forty-seven minutes from now."

"A clear pattern seems to be emerging," Michaelmas said equably.

"Damn right. But that's not the pattern I'm showing you."
"Oh?"
"Here. This is ten minutes ago. Campion's interview

technique has been to calmly move from point to point of the Norwood story, collecting answers which will be edited for sequence and time. Norwood is doing the normal amount of lip-licking, and from time to time he looks sideward to Frontiere. There's no question that any editing program worthy of the name could turn him into a semi-invalid gamely concealing his doubts. On the other hand, it could cut all that and make him sharp as the end of a pin."

"Colonel Norwood," Campion's voice said, "I'd like to follow up on that for just a moment. Now, you've just told us your flight was essentially routine until just before the explosion. But obviously you had some warning. Even an astronaut's reflexes need a little time to get him into escape mode. Could you expand on that a little? What sort of warning did you have, and how much before the explosion did it come?"

Frontiere's voice broke in. "I think perhaps that is not something you should go into at this time, Mr. Campion."

"Why not?"

"It is simply something we ought not to discuss at this time."

"I'd have to know more about that before I decided to drop the question."

"Mr. Campion, with all respect, I must insist. Now, please, back up your recording and erase that question."

There was a brief silence. Campion came in speaking slowly. "Or else our arrangement is at an end?"

Frontiere paused. "I wish you had not brought our discussion to such a juncture."

Campion abruptly said: "Someday you'll have to explain this to me. All right. Okay, crew, let's roll it back to where I asked Walt about his flight path and the last word of his answer was 'sea.' I figure a reaction shot of me, and then I frame my next question and the out-take is completely tracked over, right? That seem good to you, Clementine? Okay, Luis, we rolling back?"

Clementine's voice came in on the director track. "Roll to 'eee.' Synch. Head Campion. Roll. And."

"That's it," Domino said.

"That's what?" Michaelmas said. "Frontiere hasn't chosen to let in Campion on the telemetry sender story. Can you blame him?"

"Not my point. The unit they're using does not simply feed the director's tracking tape. It also sends direct to the EVM editing computer in Paris. No erasure took place there. The segment is already edited into the rough cut of the final broadcast. Including Norwood's sudden side glance to Frontiere, Frontiere's upset manner, and all."

Michaelmas turned his head sharply toward the window, hiding his expression in the sky. Far ahead on the right forward quarter he could see Cap Bon sliding very slowly toward the wingtip, and Tunis a white speck stabbing at his eyes in the early afternoon sun.

"He's young. It's possible he doesn't fully understand the equipment. Perhaps he thinks he did erase. It's not necessary for . ,. for any of them to know the exact nature of the equipment."

"Possibly. But Campion's contract with EVM specifies copy for simultaneous editing. He relinquished pre-editorial rights. In return for minimizing their production lag, he retains fact rights; he can use the same material as the basis for his own editions of byline book, cartridge, disc, or any other single-user package form known or to be developed during the term of copyright. And I assure you he went over every clause with EVM. He has a head for business."

"You're absolutely sure?"

"I went over it right behind him. I like to keep up with what sort of contracts are being written in our field."

"So there's no doubt he was deliberately lying to Getulio."

"None at all, Mr. Michaelmas. I'd say Campion's intention all along was to provoke something like this. He's a newsman. He smelled it out that UNAC was hiding something. He went fishing for it, and found it. When the program runs tonight, the world will know UNAC is attempting to conceal something about the shuttle accident. And of course they'll know the name of enterprising Douglas Campion."

Michaelmas put his left fist inside his cupped right hand and stared sightlessly. He patted his knuckles into his palm. "Did EVM come to him?"

"No. They were his last shot. He shopped around the US networks first. But all he'd tell anyone before signing a contract was that he thought he could get a Norwood exclusive and that he wanted to retain most of the ancillary rights. The responses he got were pretty low compared to his asking price. Then EVM picked him up. Gervaise filed an advisory to Paris. She said they'd had a conversation, and he was a good bet."

"What time was that?"

"Twelve-twenty. She'd dropped you at your hotel and apparently went straight back to hers to check out. He was waiting in the hotel, hoping she'd talk to him. He'd left a message about it for her at the desk. Obviously she and he talked. She called Paris, and then EVM's legal people called him to thrash out the contract. Everything on record is just straight business regarding quote an interview with Walter Norwood endquote."

"There was no prior agreement on slant?"

"Why should there be one? Gervaise vouched for him, and

she's respected. They take what he gives them, splice in supporting matter as it comes, and the slant develops itself. It's a hot subject, a good crew on it, and, as of a few minutes ago, no doubt in the world that they're onto something that could become notorious as hell. It's a world-class performance—a sure Pulitzer for Campion plus a dozen industry awards for the crew. It's a Nobel Laureate contender for EVM. A likely winner if the year stays slow for news."

"Well," Michaelmas said, "I suppose a man could lie to his contact for all that."

He had once seen a Chinese acrobat stack straight chairs one atop the other, balancing the rear two legs of each chair atop the backrest of the one below. The bottom chair had rested on four overturned water tumblers. The acrobat had built the stack chair by chair, while standing on each topmost chair. When the stack was twelve chairs high, the acrobat did a one-hand stand on the back of the topmost chair while rotating hoops at his ankles and free wrist. Michaelmas thought of the acrobat now, seeing him with the face of Douglas Campion.

Ten

"*Voilà* Hanrassy."

The plane slid along. "What is it, Domino?" Michaelmas palmed the bones of his face. His fingertips massaged his eyes. His thumbs pressed into his ears, trying to break some of the blockage in his eustachian tubes.

"She's placed a call to Allen Shell. She wants a scenario for telemetry- and voice-communication skewing in Norwood's shuttle."

"Ah." Shell was at MIT's Research Laboratory of Electronics. "How soon does she want it?"

"Within the hour."

"It sounds more and more as if someone's told her a tale and she's attempting to verify it."

"Exactly."

"Yes." The corners of Michaelmas's mouth pulled back

into his cheeks. He pictured Shell: a short, wiry man with a long fringe of hair and a little paunch, stumbling about his apartment and making breakfast coffee. He would probably made capuccino, assembling the ingredients and the coffeemaker clumsily, and he would take the second cup into the bathroom. Sitting on the stool with his eyes closed, sipping, he would mutter to himself in short hums through his partially compressed lips, and when he was done he would get up, find his phone where he'd left it, tell Viola Hanrassy two or three ways it might have been done undetectably, punch off, carry the empty cup and saucer to the dishwasher and very possibly drop them. Michaelmas and Shell had been classmates once. Shell had been one of the Illinois Institute of Technology students who intercepted and decoded Chicago police messages in the late 1960s, but time had passed. "Well." Michaelmas looked downward. Tunis was much larger, dimmer, and off to the right. The African coastline was falling away toward Libya, so that they would still be over water for some distance, but Cité d'Afrique was not too far ahead in time. He glanced at his wrist. They'd land at about 1400 hours local time, he judged.

"The Norwood interview's over," Domino said. "Campion did roughly the same thing a few more times. It'll be vicious when it hits."

"Yes," Michaelmas said ruminatively. "Yes, I suppose it could be." He watched the office cabin door open. The camera operator and Clementine came out. She walked with her head down, her mouth wryly twisted. She took a vacant forward seat beside her crewman and did not once glance farther up the aisle. Campion and Frontiere were lingering in the cabin doorway. Campion was thanking Frontiere, and Norwood over Frontiere's shoulder. Frontiere did not look entirely easy. When Campion turned away to come up the

156

aisle, Frontiere firmly closed the door without letting Norwood out.

Michaelmas realized Campion was deliberately heading straight for him. Campion's features had a fine sheen on them; that faint dew was the only immediate token of his past half hour's labor. But he dropped rather hard into the seat beside Michaelmas, saying, "I hope you don't mind," and then sighed. He loosened his collar and arched his throat, stroking his neck momentarily between his thumb and fingers. "Welcome to the big time, Douglas," he said in a fatigued voice.

Michaelmas smiled softly. "You're doing well, I hear."

Campion turned to him. "Coming from you, that's a real compliment." He shook his head. "I graduated today." He shook his head again, leaned back, and stretched his legs out in front of him, the heels coming down audibly. He clasped his hands at the back of his head. "It's hard, doing what we do," he reminisced, looking up at the ceiling. "I never really understood that. I used to think that doing what you did was going to be easy for me. I'd grown up with you. I knew every mannerism you have. I can do perfect imitations of you at parties." He rolled his face sideward and smiled companionably. "We all do. You know that, don't you? All us young punks."

Michaelmas shrugged with an embarrassed smile.

Campion grinned. "There must be ten thousand young Campions out there, still thinking that's all there is to it."

"There is more," Michaelmas said.

"Of course there is." Campion nodded to the ceiling. "There is," he said with his right elbow just brushing the shoulder of Michaelmas's jacket. "We're the last free people in the world, aren't we?"

"How do you mean that?"

"When I got a little older in this business, I wondered what had attracted me to it. The sophomore blahs, you know? You remember what it's like, being junior staff. Just face front and read what they give you. I used to think I was never going to get out of that. I used to think the whole world had gone to Jell-O and I was right there in the middle of it. Nothing ever happened; you'd see some movement starting up, something acting like it was going to change things in the world, and then it would peter out. Somebody'd start looking good, and then it would turn out he had more in the bank than he'd admit to, and he was allowed to graduate from his college after his father built a new gym. Or you'd want to know more about this new government program for making jobs in the city, and it would turn out to be a real estate deal.

"You began to realize the world had gotten too sophisticated for anything clear-cut to ever happen. And you know it's only the simple things that make heroes. Give you something to understand in a few words; let you admire something without holding back. Right? How are you going to feel that, when you're stuck in Jell-O and it's obviously just going to get thicker and thicker as time passes? If it wasn't for the hurricanes and the mining disasters, as a matter of fact, you might never know the difference between one day and the next.

"I almost got out of it then. Had an offer to go into PR on the governor's staff. Said no, finally. Once you're in that, you can't ever go back into news, you know? And I wasn't ready to cut it all the way off. I thought about how, when I was a kid, I thought Laurent Michaelmas *made* the news, because you were always where it was happening. And I said to myself, I'd give it one last all-the-way shot; I'd get up there

158

where you were, so I wasn't just stuck in some studio or on some payroll. Be cool, Douggie, I said to myself. Act like you're on top, aim to get on top. Get up there—get out to where they have to scurry when they see you coming, and they open the doors, and they let you see what's behind them. Get out where you rub elbows and get flown places in private equipment." Campion's eyes fastened on Michaelmas's. "That's it," he said softly. "It's not getting at the news. The news doesn't mean anything. It's being a newsman. It's getting out of the Jell-O. And now we both know that."

Michaelmas looked at him closely. "And that's what you've come to tell me," he said softly. "To get my approval."

Campion blinked. "Well, yes, if you want to put it that way." Then he smiled. "Sure! Why not? I could have a worse father figure, I guess."

"I wouldn't know about that, Douggie. But you don't need me anymore. You're a big boy now."

Campion began to smile, then frowned a little and looked sidelong at Michaelmas. He bit his lip like a man wondering if his fly had been open all along, interwove his fingers tightly before him, stiffened his arms, turned his wrists, and cracked his knuckles. He began to say something else, then frowned again and sat staring at his outthrust hands. He stood up quickly. "I have to cover a few things with those UNAC people," he said, and walked over to the bar, where he asked for Perrier water and stood drinking it through white lips.

Domino said: "Allen Shell has called Hanrassy and given her a few alternatives. One of them requires live voice from Kosmgorod and a telemetry simulating component. The

159

hardware cannot be assembled from off-the-shelf modules. It would have to be hand-built from bin parts. I imagine a knowledgeable engineer examining one could decide where its builder had gotten his technical training and done his shopping."

Which would be good enough for all practical political purposes. Michaelmas grunted. "And then what happened?"

"She put in a call for Frank Daugerd of McDonnell-Douglas. He's on a fishing vacation at the Lake of the Ozarks and has his phone holding calls, but his next check-in is due at seven AM. That will be 1400 hours at Cité d'Afrique. She's not wasting the interval. She ordered an amphibian air taxi from Lambert Field and had it dispatched down to Bagnell Dam to wait."

"Do you think she wants a second opinion on Allen's scenario?"

"I doubt it. I think she wants Daugerd to come look at some holograms from a sweetmeat store as soon as she can get him to Cape Girardeau."

"Yes. Indeed."

Daugerd was the systems interfacing man for the prime contractor on the type of module Norwood had been using. Every six or eight months, he published something that made Michaelmas sit upright and begin conversing in equations with Domino. "Well, let me see, now," Michaelmas said. "If she really does have holograms of the sender, then after he's confirmed it looks Soviet, there's only one more link to make. She'll have to determine whether Norwood really did find it aboard the module."

"Yes," Domino said bleakly. "But she may be able to do that. Then she'll brief her legislators, and they'll go to town on it. UNAC's dead by morning, and Theron Westrum may

160

as well pack his household goods. The clock's turned back twenty years."

"You really see it that way?"

"Don't you?"

It could play that way, right enough. Michaelmas smiled wistfully to himself. The way the world worked, once the word was out, the effect would take on inexhaustibility. There was always not merely the event itself, but opinion of the event, and rebuttal of the opinion, and the ready charge of self-interest, and the countercharge. There was the analysis of the event, and the excavation of the root causes of the event, and the placement of the event in the correct historical context. Everyone would want to kick the can, and it would clatter over the cobblestones interminably, far from the toes of those who'd first impelled it.

There was, for instance, the whole question of whether handsome, whip-thin Wheelwright Lundigan's narrow and unexpected victory in the 1992 Presidential election had truly represented grassroots revulsion against a decade of isolationism, or whether Lundigan-Westrum had simply been a ticket with unexpectedly strong theater. Then Lundigan's fine-boned, sharp-eyed, volatile wife had shot him through the femoral artery for good but certainly not unprecedented reasons, two months into his term. So there was also some question of whether Westrum or other sinister forces had bribed, coerced, or hypnotized her into doing it. And whether One-World Westrum was Lundigan's legitimate political heir, and then, again, what Lundigan's actual politics had been, or if in fact a majority had wanted him to have them.

None of these dilemmas had ever been truly settled—certainly not by the even slimmer election of 1996, which had gone not so much to Westrum as to his mendacious promises that he'd continue the strong-Congress-weak-President tradition, some said. Others claimed arithmetical errors in the first computer-tallied national election. Few such questions in history were ever truly settled, and here they were, all right, still not rusted away, waiting to bounce round again.

For fresher echoes, if on a lesser scale, there were nearly infinite possibilities in Hanrassy's authentication of the sender story. Shell's and Daugerd's reputations, and then those of their employers, and then those of Big Academe and Big Capital, would be at stake—and highly discussible—if the engineering scenario were questioned.

But meanwhile, Gately would be one of the first to burn to get on the air again, and, as it happened, the first open mike he'd come to would belong to EVM, which already had plenty of supporting footage showing Norwood and UNAC being appropriately evasive. It might be a little difficult to preserve a lighthearted tone while commenting on that development.

And in Moscow it would first be early evening and then night as the impact built. Once again, the managers of what was unaccountably not yet the inevitable system of the future would have to stay up late. The incredibly devious and *bieskulturni* Western nations always had the advantage of daylight. Impeccable ladies and gentlemen would have to leave off playing with their fond children after supper, or would have to forego the Bolshoi. They would hurry for the Presidium chamber, there to spell out the obvious motives behind this fantastic fabrication by the rabid forces of resurgent reaction. In dignity and full consciousness of moral superiority, with the cameras and microphones recording

162

every solemn moment of the indictment, they would let fall adjectives.

And true, Theron Westrum could forget about his so-called third term. The chances were excellent Viola Hanrassy would be the Twenty-first-century President. If that was not exactly turning back a political generation in the world, it was close enough. But in this generation the Soviets did not have so many immediate worries along their Asiatic borders to keep their pursuit of redress from being entirely single-minded. Which was a word one also applied readily to Viola. There was a hell of a lot more to her than there was to Theron, if you saw the Presidential job as defending the homestead in the forest rather than building roads to the marketplaces.

All that in the blink of an eye, Michaelmas thought. As if I had never been at all. He shook his head in wonderment. Well, there was no gainsaying it—he'd always known he was a plasterer. It would take more time than any one person was ever given to really overhaul the foundations that put the recurring cracks in the walls.

"Are you sitting there being broody again?" Domino said.

"I think I've earned the privilege."

"Well, cash it in on your own time. What's our next move?"

Michaelmas grinned. "First, I have to go to the lavatory," he said with some smugness.

But Domino followed him in. "Papashvily," he said.

Michaelmas fumbled the door lock shut. "What is it?"

"That first device was just activated. The next person entering the elevator at Papashvily's floor and selecting lobby level will have a rough ride. What has burned itself out is the circuit that dampens speed as the car approaches its stop and then aligns the car door with floor level. The passenger will be jounced severely; broken bones are a good possibility."

"What can you do?" Michaelmas worked at his clothes.

"Keep Papashvilly locked up. He hasn't found that out yet. But he will soon. Someone will come to get him."

"What activated the device?"

"I don't know. But it happened while he was ostensibly receiving an incoming call. It was from a staffer reminding him that he was expected down in the lobby when Norwood arrives. I answered it for him, but of course no one knows that. The component burned on the word 'lobby.' "

"It monitored his phone calls."

"I think so. I *think* I could design such a device; it would be a very tight squeeze."

Michaelmas pulled up his zipper. "So you weren't able to trace a signaler because there wasn't any, strictly speaking."

"The staffer may be a conspirator," Domino said dubiously. "I've checked his record. It looks clean."

"So what they've done is mined everything around Pavel, set to trigger from expectable routine events, and any one of them could plausibly cripple or kill. Sooner or later, they'll get him. And never be known, or found. That's good technology." He rinsed the soap from his hands.

"Yes."

Michaelmas shook his head. He dried his hands in the air jet, stopping while they were still a little damp and wiping his face with them. "Well, hold the fort as best you can. I'm thinking hard. So many things to keep track of," he said. "I'm glad I have you."

"Would sometimes that I had a vote in the matter. Button your coat."

When he emerged, Michaelmas said, "Look sharp" to Domino, and moved down the aisle toward the office. He passed quickly beyond Clementine's seat. The same press aide who had let him slip down the corridor at Limberg's now rose smoothly from the lounge nearest the office door. "Mr. Michaelmas," he smiled. "Signor Frontiere is in a brief meeting with Colonel Norwood. May I help you with something meanwhile?"

Michaelmas said: "UNAC hospitality is always gracious. I'm quite comfortable, thank you." He relaxed against the partition, and he and the aide exchanged pleasantries for a few score miles. Domino's terminal hung from Michaelmas's shoulder and rested flush against the bulkhead. "Harry Beloit," the aide was saying, "but I'm from Madison. My dad taught Communications at Wisconsin, and I guess it just crept into me over the dinner table." Inside the office, Norwood was saying in an insufficiently puzzled tone: "Maybe I don't understand, Getulio. But I think we should have told Campion the whole story. Hell, he's not going to be out with it until tonight. By then there's not going to be any doubt where that component came from."

Frontiere took a noticeably deep breath: "By then we will not know any more than who *seems* to have made the thing. We won't know who installed it, what they represent, or why they did it. There are many more doubts than facts, and—"

"Oh, yes, I get back as often as I can: especially in the fall. I go out to Horicon Marsh and watch the waterfowl gathering. Pack a lunch, bring along my favorite pipe, just sit with the wife on a blanket and try to teach the kids the difference between a teal and a canvasback, you know."

"—ulio, look, the only way all of these doubts of yours

165

make sense is if they expected it *not* to work. You follow me? If whoever did it was counting on my turning up with the part in my hand. I don't think they could have been counting on that. I think they expected me and it to be all blown away. So I think the people who did it are the people who look like they did it, you know?"

"They fly altogether differently. You can tell from the wingbeats when they're just coming into sight. My dad showed me."

"I've run a stress analysis on Norwood's voice. There's the overlay of irritation, of course. But he's sincere. He's completely relaxed with himself; knows who he is, what he's saying, what's right, and he's right."

"That may all be, but it is not conclusive, nevertheless. We are not going to destroy UNAC and perhaps a great deal more on the basis of a supposition. Now, in a few moments, unless I can delay long enough, you'll be speaking with Laurent Michaelmas, whom you would not be advised to underestimate, and—"

"Canada geese. They're altogether different; they're bigger, they beat slower. You know, by and large, the bigger the bird is, the less often it beats its wings. Sometimes I think that if you could see a pteranodon coming in out of the west at dusk, silhouetted against the sun, first you'd pick up the dot of its body, and then gradually you'd see little dark stubs growing out one to each side, as you began picking up the profile of the wings, and they'd never move. It would just get bigger and pick up more definition, and you'd see those motionless wings just extending themselves farther and farther out to the side, completely silent, just getting closer like it was riding a string from the top of the sky right to the bridge of your—"

"I don't think I have to make these estimates. I'm an

166

engineer, and I ran all the tests you'd want on that component. Now, I'm military, and I understand following orders, and I hope I'm capable of grasping big pictures. But there's no way you're going to get me to change my opinion on what it all means. Now, I know it's a big God-damned disappointment to you, and maybe a lot of the rest of the world, and maybe even to me. Pavel and I are good buddies, and this whole idea's had a lot of promise. But I just don't see it any way except that the boys in Moscow said, 'All right, that's long enough playing nice and catching our breath, now let's go back to doing business in the good old-fashioned way.' And I don't think it matters what you'd like to think, or I'd like to think, or how many good buddies we've got all over the world, I think we've got to face up to what really was done, and I think we've got to go from there. And damned quick."

"Nevertheless, until superior authority tells you what is to be done—"

"Yes, sir, for as long as I'm detailed to serve under that authority, that's exactly correct."

"Signals. You know, everything that lives is constantly sending out signals. My dad pointed that out to me. It's how animals teach and control their young, it's how they mate, it's how they move in groups from place to place. They've got these fantastic vocabularies of movement, cry, and odor. Any member of any species knows them all. It can recognize its own kind when you'd swear there was nothing out there, and it knows immediately whether that other creature is sick or well, at rest or frightened, feeding or searching, or whatever."

"Mr. Michaelmas, he's going to resign and talk if he gets no satisfaction."

"Yes."

"They know all of that about each other all the time. I guess that's about all there is to know in this world, really. Seems a shame the animal that signals the most seems to need individuals like me to help it along, and even so—"

"Even so," Michaelmas said. "Even so, we're the only animal whose signals can't be trusted by its own kind." He smiled. "Except for thee and me, of course."

Harry Beloit smiled with awkward kinship. Then the plane tilted and he glanced out a window. "We'll be in the Afrique approach pattern in a few moments," he said. "I'm sorry—it seems as if Signor Frontiere's and Colonel Norwood's conference took longer than expected."

"No matter," Michaelmas said equably. "I'll catch them in the limousine." He waved a hand gently and turned. "Ours was a pleasant conversation." He moved up the aisle until he reached Clementine. Putting one buttock on the armrest of the seat across the aisle, he smiled at her. She had been sitting with her eyes down, her lips a little pursed and grim. "A pleasant flight?" he said politely.

Domino snorted.

Clementine looked up at Michaelmas. "It's a very comfortable aircraft."

"How do you find working with Campion?"

She raised an eyebrow. "One is a professional." It had very much been not the sort of question one is asked.

"Of course," Michaelmas said. "I don't doubt it. Since this morning I've made it my business to look into your career. Your accomplishments bear out my personal impression."

She smiled with a touch of the wistful. "Thank you. It's a day-to-day thing, however, isn't it? You can't remain still if you wish to advance."

He smiled "No. No, of course not. But you seem well

168

situated. A very bright star in a rapidly growing organization, and now in one day you have credits with me and with a rising personality, both on a major story. . . ."

"Yes, he is rising overnight," Clementine said, unconsciously jerking her head toward the back of the plane. "Not a Campion but a mushroom," she said in French.

Michaelmas smiled. Then he giggled. He found he could not control it. Little tears came to his eyes. Domino said. "Stop that! Good heavens!"

Clementine was staring at him, her hand masking her mouth, her own shoulders shaking. "Incredible! You look like the little boy when the schoolmaster trips."

He still could not bring himself to a halt. "But you, my dear, are the one who soaped the steps."

They laughed together, as decorously as possible, until they had both run down and sat gasping. It was incredible how relieved Michaelmas felt. He was completely unconcerned that people up the aisle were staring at them, or that Luis, the camera operator, sat beside Clementine stiffly looking out the window like a gentleman diner overhearing a jest between waiters.

Finally, Clementine dabbed under her eyes with the tips of her fingers and began delving into her purse. She said: "Ah. Ah, Laurent, nevertheless," more soberly now, "this afternoon there's been something I could have stopped. You'll see it tonight and say, 'Here something was done that she could surely have interrupted, if she weren't so professional.'" She opened her compact and touched her cheeks with a powder pad. She looked up and sideward at Michaelmas. "But it is not professional of me to say so. We have shocked Luis."

The camera operator's lip twitched. He continued to stare

out his window with his jaw in his palm. "I do not listen to private conversations," he said correctly. "Especially not about quick-witted people who instruct in technique to something they call 'crew.'"

Michaelmas grinned. "*Viva* Luis," he said softly. He put his hand on Clementine's wrist and said: "Whatever was done—do you think it serves the truth?"

"Oh, the truth, yes," Clementine said.

"She means it, Domino said. "She's a little elevated, but simple outrage would account for that. There's no stab of guilt."

"Yes, her pulse didn't change," Michaelmas said to him, bending over Clementine's hand to make his farewell. He said to her: "Ah, well, then, whatever else there is, is bearable. I had best sit down somewhere now." Campion would be back down here in a minute, ready to discuss what was to be done as soon as they landed. "*Au revoir.*"

"*Certainement.*"

"Daugerd checked his phone early," Domino said. "It's a terrible day for fishing; pouring rain. He's returned Hanrassy's call; she had something that needs his professional appraisal. He's running his bass boat down to the Bagnell Dam town landing to meet that plane of hers. Bass boats are fast. His ETA at her property will be something like seven-forty her time—about half an hour after you deplane at Cité d'Afrique."

Michaelmas touched his lips to the back of Clementine's hand, feeling the fragility of the bones, and moved up the aisle. Campion watched him warily.

"Sincere, you say," Michaelmas said to Domino as he dropped into a seat. "Norwood."

"Absolutely. I wish I had that man's conscience."

170

"Do you suppose," Michaelmas ventured, "that something is bringing in people from a parallel world? Eh?" He stared out the window, his jaw in his palm, as the coast slid below them. The Mediterranean was not blue but green like any other water, and the margins of the coast were so rumpled into yellow shallows and bars that on this surfless day it was almost impossible to decide whether they would fall on land or water. "You know the theory? Every world event produces alternative outcomes? There is a world in which John Wilkes Booth missed and Andrew Johnson was never President, so there was much less early clamor for threatening Nixon with impeachment? So he didn't name Jerry Ford, but someone else, instead? The point being that Lincoln never knew he was dead, and Ford never dreamed he'd been President."

"I know that concept," Domino said shortly. "It's sheer anthropomorphism."

"Hmm. I suppose. Yet he *is* sincere, you tell me."

"Hold his hand."

Michaelmas smiled off-center. "He's dead."

"How?"

The landing warnings came on. Michaelmas adjusted his seat and his belt.

"I don't know, friend ... I don't know," he mused. He continued to stare out the window as the plane settled lower with its various auxiliaries whining and thumping. The wings extended their flaps and edge-fences in great sooty pinions; coronal discharges flickered among the spiny deperturbance rakes. "I don't know ... but then, if God had really intended Man to think, He would have given him brains, I suppose."

"Oh, wow," Domino said.

They swept in over the folded hills that protected Cité

171

d'Afrique from serious launch pad errors at Star Control. To Michaelmas's right, the UNAC complex was a rigid arrangement pile-driven into the desert; booster sheds, pads, fuel dumps, guidance bunkers, and the single prismatic tower where UNAC staff dwelled and sported and took the elevators down or up to their offices or the lobby. The structures seemed isolated: menhirs erected on a plain once green, now the peculiar lichenous shade of scrubby desert, very much like the earliest television color pictures of the Moon. These were connected to each other by animal trails which were in fact service roads, bound to the hills by the highway cutting straight for Cité d'Afrique, and, except for that white and sparsely traveled lifeline, adrift—probably clockwise, like the continent itself. Beyond it there was only a browning toward sand and a chasming toward sky, and Saint-Exupéry flying, flying, straining his ears to filter out the sound of the slipstream in his guy wires, listening only to the increasingly harsh sound of engine valves laboring under a deficiency of lubricating oil, wiping his goggles impatiently and peering over the side of the cockpit for signs of life.

Michaelmas looked down at his quiescent hands.

Now they were over the hills, and then the ground dropped sharply. Cité d'Afrique opened before them. The sunlight upon it was like the scimitars of Allah. It was all a tumble of shahmat boards down there: white north surfaces, all other sides energy-absorbent black, metallized glass lancing reflections back at catcher panels, louvers, shadow banners, clash of metal chimes, street cries, robed men like knights, limousine horns, foreigners moving diagonally, the bazaar smell newly settled into recently wet mortar but not quite yet victorious over aldehydes outbaking from the plastics, and Konstantinos Cikoumas. Michaelmas saw him as

172

a tall, cadaverous, round-eyed, open-mouthed man in a six-hundred-dollar suit and a grocer's apron with a screwdriver in its bib pocket. He did not see where Cikoumas was or what he was doing at the moment, and he could not guess what the man thought.

They had made Cité d'Afrique in no longer than it takes to pull the UN out of New York and decree a new city. Not as old as the youngest of sheikhs, it was the new cosmopolitan center. Its language was French because the men with hawk faces knew French as the diplomatic and banking language of the world, but it was not a French city, and its interests were not confined to those of Africa. It was, the UN expected, a harbinger of a new world. Eloquent men had ventured to say that only by making a place totally divorced from nationalistic pressures could the United Nations function as required, and so they had moved here.

Michaelmas asked Domino: "What's the situation at the terminal?"

"There's a fair amount of journalist activity. They have themselves set up at the UNAC gate. You hired the best local crew, and they know the ropes, so they're situated at a good angle. EVM has a local man there to shoot backup footage of Norwood debarking. Then there are UNAC people at the gate, of course, to welcome Norwood, although none of them are very high up the ladder, and there are curious members of the public—mostly UN personnel and diplomats who got early word Norwood was coming in by this route. And so forth."

"Very good. Uh, we may be calling upon your Don't Touch circuit sometime along in there."

"Oh, really?" Domino said.

"Yes. I believe I have taken an instructive lesson from the

173

Ecole Psychologique of Marseilles. Other topic: Do you have a scan on where Konstantinos Cikoumas lives?"

"Certainly. A nice modern apartment with a view of the sea. Nothing exceptional in it. Nothing like the stuff planted all over Star Control. But then, why should they risk Kosta's ever being tied to any exotic machinery that might accidentally be found in the vicinity? He and his brother are honest merchants, after all, and who's to ever say different? Kristiades called him this afternoon, by the way. At about the time we left Berne. A routine talk concerning almonds. It doesn't yield to cryptanalysis. But the fact of the call itself may be his way of saying Norwood's enroute, meaning there'll be plenty of press to cover any accidents to Papashvilly."

"You'd think," Michaelmas grumbled, "UNAC might look more deeply at who comes and goes through Star Control."

"They do. They think they do. But they don't think in terms of this sort of attack. They think in terms of someone ripping off souvenirs or trying to sell insurance; maybe an occasional lone flat-Earther; maybe someone who'd like to be an ardent lover. Look what they've done—they've put Papashvilly in his own apartment, which they consider is secure, which it is, and fully private, and they've left him alone. He's playing belly-dance recordings and drinking Turkish coffee, oblivious as a lamb."

Michaelmas snorted. "He eats lamb. But something's got to be done; they're piling trash all around my ability to concentrate." He blinked vigorously, sitting up in his seat, and rubbed his eyes, now that he'd remembered himself. He felt the taste of verdigris far back on his tongue, and growled softly to himself. Except that Domino overheard it, of cours. . There is no God-damned *privacy!* he thought. None whatever. Any day now, he decided, Domino's receptor in his skull would begin being able to receive harmonics from his brain electrical activity, and then it would be just a matter of time before they became readable. *Merde!* he cried in his mind, and hurled something down a long, narrowing dark hallway. "All right. Are you sure you've found all the little gimmicks around Papashvilly?"

"I've swept the main building, and everything else Papashvilly might approach. I'm fairly certain I have them. I don't understand," Domino said peevishly, "where they got so many of them, or who thought of them, or why this technique. It seems to me they'd want to plant one good bomb and get it over with."

"Not if what they want to kill is the whole idea of effective astronautics. They don't want isolated misfortunes. They want a pattern of wrangling and doubt. They want to roil up the world's mind on the subject. Damn them, they're trying to gnaw the twentieth century to death. They just don't want us poking around the Solar System. Their Solar System? Any ideas along those lines?"

"I believe they are the descendants of the lost Atlantean civilization," Domino said. "Returning from their former interstellar colonies and battling for their birthright. It seems only fair."

"Very good. Now, the gadgets. Do you understand what each of those gadgets could do?"

"I think so. There's a nearly infinite variety. Some will start fires and cut off the adjacent heat sensors simultaneously. Others will most likely do things such as overloading Papashvilly's personal car steering controls—at a moderate speed if you're right, at a higher one if you're not. The elevator you know about. There's something I think will cut

175

out the air-conditioning to his block of flats, probably at the same time the night-heater thermostat oversets. If I were doing it, that would also be the time the fire doors all dropped shut, sealing off that wing with him inside it, at, say, 110 degrees Fahrenheit. Should I go on?"

"That will do for samples. Are all of these pieces wired into the building circuits?"

"All that aren't concerned with free-standing machinery like the car. They're all perfect normal-acting components— with a plus."

"All right. I've been thinking. You could trip them, couldn't you? You tested that elevator part."

"Right," Domino said slowly. "I could. Use the building systems to give 'em an overload jolt of current. That would fry 'em as surely as their own triggers could."

Michaelmas steepled his fingertips. "Well, that's all right, then. How's this for a sequence: At the appropriate time, Pavel gets a call to come down to the lobby. You let his door open. He goes out in the hall, and the tampered elevator won't open its doors; you can do that through the normal systems. So he has to take another. Make sure it's a clean one. Meanwhile, you're tidying up behind him. As soon as he clears each problem area, you blow each of the gimmicks in it. By the time he's down to ground level, the building will be safe for him. A little disarranged, but safe. A priority repair order to the garage systems ties up his car, should he get it into his head to go for a spin. Et cetera. Good scenario?"

Domino made a peculiar noise. "Oh, my, yes. Can do. When do you want it?"

"When appropriate. UNAC will surely call him to come down when Norwood is almost there. Initiate it then."

"All right."

176

"And Konstantinos Cikoumas. Let him get a call from a UNAC functionary right away, inviting him to join the greeters at the airport gate."

"No problem."

"Excellent. He has plenty of gates and things to pass through as he approaches the debarking ramp, right? Heat locks, friskers, and so forth."

"It's a hot country. And it's an ultramodern airport, yes."

"Make sure he has no difficulty arriving at the last gate exactly on time, will you?"

"No problem. He's already left his apartment; I'm monitoring his cab's dispatch link. And I can help or hinder with the traffic signals."

"There, now," Michaelmas said with a sigh. "Remember, he's coming through the last gate as Norwood arrives."

"Absolutely," Domino made the noise again; this time, he seemed to manage it a little better.

Michaelmas ignored it. He took a deep breath and settled back in his seat. "Pillar to post," he muttered. "Pillar to post."

The plane flared out past the outer marker, and Michaelmas folded his hands loosely in his lap. In a few moments it was down, tires thumping as the thin air marginally failed to provide a sufficient cushion. There were the usual roarings and soft cabin chimes, and surging apparent alterations in the direction his body wanted to go. There was a sharp change in the smell of the cabin as the air-conditioning sucked in the on-shore breeze, chilled it, and the relative humidity rose thirty percent in an instant.

"Frank Daugerd is airborne from the Lake of the Ozarks," Domino said. "His pilot has filed an ETA of 07:35, their time. That's thirty-three minutes from now."

"And then . . . let's see. . . ." Michaelmas rubbed his nose; his sinuses were stuffed. He grimaced and counted it up in his head: the touchdown on the Mississippi, floats pluming the water, and the drift down to the landing. The waiting USA staffer with the golf cart, and the silent, gliding run from the landing up the winding crushed-shell drive to the east portico; the doors opening, and Daugerd disappearing inside, hunched and busy, still wearing his fishing vest and hat, probably holding his hand over the bowl of his pipe; the conversation with Hanrassy, the bending over the table, the walking around the holograms, the snap decision and then the thoughtful review of the decision, the frowning, the looking closer, and then, for good and all, the nod of confirmation, the farewell handshake with Hanrassy, the departure from the room, and Hanrassy reaching for her telephone. "Ten minutes? Fifteen? Between the time he lands at her dock and the time she reacts to a confirmation?"

"Yes," Domino said. "That's how I count it. Adding it all up, fifty minutes from now, all she'll have left to do is call Gately and have him call Norwood. He gets through where she couldn't, he asks Norwood the direct question, Norwood gives the direct answer, Gately's back on the phone to Hanrassy, and Bob's your uncle. One hour from now, total, it's all over."

"Ah, if men had the self-denial of Suleiman the Wise," Michaelmas said, "to flask the clamorous djinns that men unseal."

"What's *that* from?"

"From me. I just made it up. These things come to my mind. Isn't it bloody awful?" He winced; his voice seemed to echo through the back of his neck and rebound from the inner surfaces of his eardrums. The price of wit.

178

A cabin attendant said nasally over the PA: "We shall be at the UNAC deplaning area shortly. Please retain your seats until we have come to a complete stop."

Michaelmas unclenched his hands, opened his seatbelt, rose, and moved deftly down the aisle. He passed between Campion and Clementine, and dropped lightly into the forward seat beside Harry Beloit. "I'll just want a word with Getulio before we get into all the bustle at the terminal," he said. "That'll be possible, won't it?" He smiled engagingly.

Beloit returned the smile. "No problem." He understood. Whatever Michaelmas might say to Getulio at this point was irrelevant. The famous newsman simply needed a reason to be with Frontiere at the deplaning, since Norwood would also be kept in close proximity, and therefore all three of them would be on camera together at the arrival gate. That would include Campion's camera. There was such a thing as giving ground in a statesmanly manner while the plane was in the air and Campion had first call on the astronaut's time. There was another thing entirely in being upstaged before the world.

Beloit smiled again, fondly. Even the greatest were as transparent as children, and he clearly loved them for it.

Michaelmas's head cocked and turned as he peered through the windows at the approaching terminal buildings; he felt the reassuring rumble of wheels on concrete, and his eyes sparkled.

"How much Don't Touch are we going to need?" Domino was saying to him.

"Just enough to twitch a muscle," Michaelmas replied. "On request or on the word 'crowded.'"

" 'Crowded.' Good enough," Domino said. "Are you sure you don't want to go heavier than that?"

179

Every so often, the idly curious person or the compulsive gadget-tryer wandered over to where the terminal might be lying, and began poking at it. A measured amount of this was all to the good, but it was not something to be encouraged. There were also occasional times when the prying was a little more purposeful, although of course one did not lightly ascribe base motives to one's fellow news practitioners. And conceivably there might be a time when the sternest measures were required.

The terminal operated on six volts DC, but it incorporated an oscillator circuit that leaked into the metal case when required to do so. It was possible to deliver a harmless little thrum, followed by Michaelmas's solicitous apology for the slight malfunction. It was also possible to throw someone, convulsive and then comatose, to the floor. In such cases, more profuse reaction from Michaelmas and a soonest-possible battery replacement were required.

"It will do."

"But if you're going to topple Norwood on camera, you'll want the effect to be dramatic. You'll want to make sure the world can readily decide he isn't really one hundred percent sound."

"We are not here to trick the world into an injustice," Michaelmas said, "nor to excessively distress a sincere man. Please do as I say, when said."

"At times you're difficult to understand."

"Well, there's good and bad in that." Michaelmas's gaze had returned to Harry Beloit. He smiled at Harry fondly.

Eleven

Michaelmas and Frontiere stood watching the approach of the umbilical corrider from the gate. "Is it going well?" Michaelmas asked politely.

Frontiere glanced aside at Norwood, who was chatting casually with some of the UNAC people while Luis worked his camera, and then at Campion, who was close behind Luis's shoulder. "Oh, yes, it's fine," he said.

Michaelmas smiled faintly. "My sympathies. May I ride to Star Control in the same vehicle with you and Norwood?"

"Certainly. We are all going in an autobus in any case; we are very proud of the latest Mercedes, which incorporates a large number of our accumulator patents. Accordingly, we have a great many of the vehicles here, and use them at every opportunity, including the photographable ones." Frontiere's thinned lips twisted at the corners. "It was my suggestion. I work indefatigably on my client's behalf." He glanced at Campion again. "Perhaps a little too much sometimes."

Michaelmas clapped him on the shoulder. "Be at your ease, Getulio. You are an honest man, and therefore invulnerable."

"Please do not speak in jest, my friend. There is a faint smell here, and I am trying to convince myself none of it comes from me."

"Ah, well, things often right themselves if a man only has patience." Michaelmas caught Clementine's eye as she stood back beyond Campion and Luis. She had been watching Campion steer Luis's elbow. Michaelmas smiled at her, and she shook her head ruefully at him. He winked, and turned back to Frontiere. "Have you heard from Ossip? How are the verification tests on the sender?"

Frontiere shrugged. "I have not heard. He was only about an hour ahead of us in bringing it here. The laboratory will be proceeding carefully."

Norwood's voice rose a little. He was making planar patterns in the air, his hands flattened, and completing a humorous anecdote from his test-flying days. His eyes sparkled, and his head was thrown back youthfully. You'd trust your life's savings to him. "Very carefully," Frontiere said at Michaelmas's shoulder, "if they hope to contradict him convincingly."

"Cheer up, Getulio," Michaelmas said. "The workmanship only looks Russian. In fact, it comes from a small Madagascan supplier of Ukrainian descent whose total output is pledged to the Laccadive Antiseparatist Crusade. Or in fact the false voice transmissions did not come from Kosmgorod. No, by coincidence they emanated from an eight-armed

182

amateur radio hobbyist just arriving from Betelgeuse in its spacetime capsule. It has no interest in this century or the next, and is enroute to setting up as a god in pre-Columbian Peru."

"Right," Domino said.

The umbilical arrived at the aircraft hatch and locked on. A cabin attendent pushed open the door. Michaelmas took a deep, surreptitious breath. The little interlude between taxiing to the pad and the arrival of the corridor had ended. Frontiere shook his head at Michaelmas. "Come along, Laurent," he said. "I wish I had your North American capacity for humor." They moved into the diffused pale lighting and the cold air.

Waiting for them was the expected thicket of people who really had no business being there, as well as those with credentials or equally plausible excuses. They were being held back behind yielding personnel barriers, and up to now they had stood in more or less good order, rubbing expensively-clad shoulders discreetly, each conscious of dignity and place, each chatting urbanely with the next.

But when the debarking corridor doors opened, they forgot. They became fixated on the slim man with the boy face, and there was nothing tailoring or other forms of sophistication could do about that.

Norwood. It was, indeed, Norwood. Ah.

They moved forward, and where the barriers stopped them, they unhooked them automatically, without looking, staring straight ahead.

"On your diagonal right," Domino said, and Michaelmas broke off staring at the welcomers and looked. A tall, cadaverous young man in an Alexandria-tailored yellow suit was coming through the second of the automatic clamshell doors into the area. His large, round brown eyes were sparkling. He strode boldly, and he had his thumbs hooked into the slash pockets of his weskit. "Cikoumas."

"Bust him," Michaelmas said.

The doors nipped the hurrying young man's heel. He cried out and pitched forward, arms flailing. His attempt to get at least one elbow down did not succeed; his nose struck heavily into the stiff pile of the carpeting. He struggled face-down, cursing, one foot held high between the doors, but only a security guard moved toward him with offers of assistance and promises of infirmary. He was, after all, at the back of the crowd.

Brisk in the air-conditioning, jockeying for position, the aircraft passengers proceeded to the gate, where cameras, microphones and dignitaries did their work, but not as smoothly as the UNAC press people, who lubricated the group through its passage toward the ground-vehicle dock. Camera crews eddied around the main knot of movement. "The dignified gentleman with the rimless glasses is Mr. Raschid Samir, your director," Domino said. Mr. Samir was directing general shots of Michaelmas debarking with Norwood and Frontiere. He had an economy of movement and a massive imperturbability which forced others to work around him as if he were a rock in the rapids. "He will follow you to Star Control with the crew truck and await instructions."

Michaelmas nodded. "Right. Good." As they moved out of the terminal building proper, he was concentrating on his position in the crowd while plotting all the vectors on Norwood. Two crews at the nearer end of the dock were covering most of one side of the astronaut as he strode along, grinning and still shaking hands with some of the local

184

UNAC people. Frontiere was staying close to him, thus blanketing most of his right flank. Other camera positions or live observers were covering the other approach angles almost continuously. Michaelmas stepped sideward in relation to a group of press aides moving along beside Campion and Clementine. While they masked him from forward view, he shifted the strap of the terminal from his left shoulder into his hand, and then stepped behind a dockside pillar. The bus was there, snugged into its bay, white and black, the roof chitinous with accumulators, the windows polarized, the doors folding open now while the party rippled to a halt. Norwood half turned, directly in front of Michaelmas, almost in the doorway, tossing a joke back over his shoulder, one hand on an upright metal stanchion, as the group narrowed itself down to file in. Michaelmas was chatting with a press aide. "We're crowded here, aren't we?" he remarked, and laid a corner of the dangling terminal up against Norwood's calf muscle just below the back of the knee, so gently, so surely, so undetectably that he half expected to hear the pang of a harmonic note. But instead Norwood sagged just a little on that side before his hand suddenly gripped the stanchion whitely, and his toe kicked the step riser. His eyes widened at betrayal. He moved on, and in, and sat down quickly in the nearest of the individual swiveling arm chairs. As the bus filled and closed, and then rolled out through the insulated gates, Michaelmas could see him chatting and grinning but flexing the calf again and again, as if it were a sweet wife who'd once kissed a stranger. I could have done worse by you, Michaelmas thought, but it was nevertheless unpleasant to watch the trouser fabric twitching.

The bus rolled smoothly along the ramps among the towers, aiming for the hills and then Star Control. "Would

185

you like to speak to Norwood now?" Frontiere asked, leaning across the aisle. "We will arrive at quarter to three, so there is half an hour."

Michaelmas shook his head. "No, thank you, Getulio," he smiled, making himself look a little wan. "I think I'll rest a bit. It's been a long day. I'll catch him later."

"You look tired," Frontiere agreed, annoyingly.

Michaelmas cocked an eyebrow. "Let Campion continue to interview him. There must be one or two things he would still like to know."

Frontiere winced. "Listen," he said softly, "you say Campion has a good reputation?"

"I say, and so do others whose judgment I respect. He has a fine record for aggressive newsgathering."

Frontiere nodded to himself, faintly, wryly, and grunted. "Somehow, that's small comfort."

"It's the best I can do," Michaelmas said. Down the aisle, Clementine had turned her seat to form a conversational group with Luis and Campion. Campion was talking intently. Clementine was responding and gesturing, her hands held forward and curved inward to describe shots, in the manner that made all directors resemble Atlas searching for a place to rest his burden. Luis sat back, his arms folded across his chest. Michaelmas reclined lower in his seat. "I would like to see Papashvilly as soon as possible after we reach Control. My crew chief is Mr. Raschid Samir, and he'll be arriving by truck at the same time."

"Yes, that's arranged. Pavel is waiting for you. He says to meanwhile tell you the story about the aardvark and Marie Antoinette."

"It's the same as the story about the aardvark and Isadora Duncan, except that the Isadora Duncan version is better, since she is wearing a long scarf at the time."

"Ah."

"And could you let me know if you hear from Ossip about the sender?"

"On the instant."

"*Grazie.*" Michaelmas settled his head deeper between the sound-absorbent wings of his chair and closed his eyes.

Domino said: "The joke about the aardvark and Isadora Duncan is the same as the joke about the aardvark and Annie Oakley, except that Annie is firing a Sharps repeating carbine."

"Granted," Michaelmas said absently. He was comfortable and relaxed, and remembering Pavel Papashvily in the back room of a chophouse around the corner from Cavanaugh's, down on lower Eighth Avenue, after a recording at Lincoln Center.

"Cosmonautics and culture," Papashvily was saying, leaning back on a fauteuil with his arm lightly across the shoulders of a member of the corps de ballet, "how allied!" The footage had been of Papashvily at *Coppelia*, first walking at night like a demon of the steppes among the floodlit fountains of the plaza, afraid of nothing, a meter and a half in height, eyes flickering with reflections, grinning. The pause at the great glass doors, the head tilted upward, and the photosensitive mechanism swinging them apart without further human intervention. Now the click of heels on marble gave way to orchestrated music, and the opening credits and title came up. Then at the performance he had smiled and oohed and aahed, hands elevated and tracing patterns in the air, and he had stood and applauded and shouted. Now he passed a palm delicately along wispy fabric at the dancer's pale shoulder. "What thin partitions," he murmured, winking at Michaelmas. He laughed, the dancer gave him a knowing sidelong look, and they all three had a

187

little more steak and lobster and some more Rhine wine. "That will be a good thing, this program," Pavel said. "This is a good thing, this visit. I know you American people are disappointed about Walter." He paused and took a sip, his lips pressed hard against the rim of the glass, his eyes looking off into a dimmer corner of the little room. "It was a stupid, needless thing, whatever happened. We are not after all any longer doing things for the first or second time, correct? But it is now for an understanding to be made that he and I and all the others, we are for all the people." He put the glass down and considered. "And we are from all the people," he had added, and Michaelmas had smiled a little crookedly. When he had seen the dancer's hand on Pavel's thigh, he had excused himself and gone home.

The UNAC bus passed from the last tangle of feeder ramps and entered the straightline highway into the hills. There was no speed limit on this road; the passenger chairs moved a little on their gymbals as the acceleration built. A nearly inaudible singing occurred in Michaelmas's ear; something in the system somewhere was cycling very near the frequency he and Domino used between him and the terminal. A mechanic had failed to lock some service hatch. Noise leaked out of the propulsion bay. Michaelmas grimaced and ground his teeth lightly.

Coarse, scoured, and ivory-colored in the sun beyond the windows, the foothills rose under the toned blue of the sky.

Norwood had stopped fussing with his leg. But he had also stopped being so animated, and was sitting with one corner of his lip pulled into his teeth, thoughtfully.

There had been a time a little later in the US tour, at a sports-car track in the gravel hills of eastern Long Island. Rudi Cherpenko had been conducting some tire tests, and offered Papashvilly a ride if he had time. UNAC had thought it a fine idea, if Michaelmas or someone of that stature would cover it. Pavel had taken once around the track to learn how to drift and how to steer with the accelerator, and half around to learn how to brake and to deduce good braking points, and by then his adrenalin was well up. He went around five times more; he could be seen laughing and shouting in the cockpit as he drilled past the little cluster of support vehicles. When he was finally flagged off, he came in flushed and large-eyed, trembling. "Oy ah!" he had shouted, vaulting out of the cockpit. *"Jiesus Maria,* what a thing this is to do!" He jumped at Cherpenko. They guffawed and embraced, slamming their hands down between each other's shoulderblades with the car's engine pinging and contracting beside them as it cooled. Yet Michaelmas had caught the onset of sobriety in Papashvilly's eyes. He was laughing and shaking his head, but when he saw that Michaelmas was seeing the change in him, he returned a little flicker of a rueful smile.

Late that night in the rough-timbered bar of the Inn, with Cherpenko asleep in his room because of the early schedule, and the crew people off raising hell on Shelter Island, Papashvilly had sat staring out the window, beyond the reflection of their table candle, and beyond the silhouettes of docked cabin boats. Michaelmas had listened.

"It is an intoxication," Papashvilly had begun. As he went on, his voice quickened whenever he pictured the things he talked about, slowed and lowered when he explained what they meant. "It takes hold."

Michaelmas smiled. "And you are back in the days of George the Resplendent?"

Papashvilly turned his glance momentarily sideward at

189

Michaelmas. He laughed softly. "Ah, George Lasha of the Bagratid Empire. Yes, a famous figure. No, I think perhaps I go back farther than eight hundred years. You call me Georgian. In the Muscovite language, I am presumed a Gruzian. Certain careless speakers from my geographic area yet refer to Sakartvelo, the united kingdom. Well, some of us are very ambitious. And I cannot deny that in my blood there is perhaps some trace of the great Kartlos, and that I am of the eastern kingdom, that is, a Kartvelian."

He was drinking gin, as an experiment. He raised his glass, wrinkled his nose, swallowed and smiled at the window. "There have been certain intrusions on the blood since even long before the person you call Alexsandr the Great came with his soldiers to see if it was true about the golden fleece, when Sakartvelo was the land of Colchis. I am perhaps a little Mingrelian, a little Kakhetian, a little Javakhete, a little Mongol . . ." He put his hand out flat, thumb and palm down, and trembled it slightly. "A little of this and that." He closed his fist. "But my mother told me on her knee that I am an Ossete of the high grassy pastures, and we were there before anyone spoke or wrote of any other people in those highlands. We have never relinquished them. No, not to the Turks, not to Timur the Lame and his elephants, nor to the six-legged Mongols. It was different, of course, in the low-lands, though those are stout men." He nodded to himself. "Stout men. But they had empires and relinquished them."

He put down his glass again and held it as if to keep it from rising, while he looked at it inattentively. "To the south of us is a flood of stone—the mountain, Ararat, and the Elburz, and Iran, and Karakorum, and Himalaya. To the north of us is the grass that rolls from the eastern world and breaks against the Urals. To the east and west of us are seas like walls; it is the grass and stone that toss us on their surf. Hard men from the north seek Anatolia and the fat sultanates. Hard men from the south seek the Khirgiz pasturage and the back door to Europe. Two thousand years and more we clung to our passes and raided from our passes, becoming six-legged in our turn, until the sultans tired, and until the Ivan Grodznoi, whom you call The Terrible, with his cannon crushed the Mongols of the north." Papashvilly nodded again. "And so he freed his race that Timur-i-leng created and called slaves—" Papashvilly shrugged. "Perhaps they are free forever. Who knows? Time passes. We look south, we look north, we see the orchards, we smell the grass. Our horses canter and paw the air. But we cling, do we not, because the age of the six-legged is over, is it not? Now we are a Soviet Socialist Republic and we have the privilege of protecting Muscovy from the south. Especially since Josef. Perversity! Our children have the privilege of going to Muscovite academies if we are eligible, and . . ." He put his hand on Michaelmas's forearm. "But of how much interest is this to you? In your half of the world, there is of course no history. One could speak to the Kwakiutl or the Leni-Lenape and the Apache, I suppose, but they have twice forgotten when they were six-legged people and they do not remember the steppes. No, you understand without offense, Lavrenti, that there is enough water between this land and the land of your forefathers to dissolve the past for you, but where I was born there has been so much blood and seed spilled on the same ground over and over that sometimes there are new men, they say, who are found in the pastures after the fog: men who go about their business unspeaking, and without mothers."

Papashvilly put down his empty glass. "Do they have

coffee here with whiskey in it? I think I like that better. Ah, this business with the sports car. . . ." He shook his head. "You know, it is true: all we peoples who live by the horse—not your sportsmen or your hobbyists, not anyone who is free to go elsewhere and wear a different face—we say that man is six-legged who no longer counts the number of his legs. But this is not love of the animal; it is love of the self as the self is made greater, and why hide it? Let me tell you how it must be—ah, you are a man of sharp eyes, I think you know how it is: On the grass ocean there are no roads, so everything is a road, and everything is the same, so the distances will eat your heart unless you are swift, swift, and shout loud. I think if Dzinghiz Khan—I give him this, the devil, they still speak his name familiarly even on the Amber Sea—if the Dzinghiz Khan had been shown an armored car, there would have been great feasts upon horseflesh in that season, and thereafter the fat cities would have been taxed by the two-hundred-liter drum. The horse is a stubborn, dirty, stupid animal that reminds me of a sheep. Its only use is to embody the wings a man feels within him, and to do this it lathers and sweats, defecates and steps in badger holes."

Then he had smiled piercingly. "But really, it is the same with cars, too." His voice was soft and sober. "I would not like Rudi to hear me say that. He's a good fellow. But it's also the same with rockets. If you have wings inside, nothing is really fast enough. You do the best you can, and you shout loud."

They were well into the hills, now. Campion was smiling at Norwood and trying to get him into conversation. Norwood was shaking his head silently. Clementine was stretched out in her seat, sipping through a straw at an ice from the refreshment bar, raising one eyebrow as she chatted with Luis. It seemed reasonable to suppose they had been a great many places together. Michaelmas grimaced and closed his eyes again.

There was the night before the goodwill visit was at an end and Papashvilly was due to be at Star Control the next day. There had been a long, wet dinner at the Rose Room, and then they had gone for a constitutional along Fifth Avenue in the middle of the night. As they stepped off a curb, a fast car had turned a corner tightly, with no regard to them. Michaelmas had scrambled back with a shout to Papashvilly. Pavel had stopped still, allowing the rear fender to pass him by millimeters. As it passed, he brought down his fist hard on the rear deck sheet-metal with an enormous banging sound that echoed between the faces of the stores. The security escort out in the shadows had pointed their guns and the camera crews had jolted their focus. The car had screamed to a halt on locked wheels, slewing sideward, and the driver's window had popped open to reveal a pale, frightened, staring face. "Earthman!" Papashvilly had shouted, his fists clenched. His knees and elbows were bent. His head thrust forward on his corded neck. "Earthman!" But he was beginning to laugh, and he was relaxing. He walked forward and rumpled the driver's hair fondly. "Ah, earthman, earthman, you are only half drunk." He turned away and continued down the avenue.

They had walked a little more, and then they had all gone back toward the hotel for a night cap. At the turn onto Forty-fourth Street, Papashvilly had stopped for a moment and looked around. "Goodbye, Fifth Avenue," he said.

193

"Goodbye library, goodbye Rockefeller Center, goodbye cathedral, goodbye Cartier, goodbye F.A.O. Schwarz, goodbye zoo."

Michaelmas looked up and down the avenue with him, and nodded.

Sitting alone together in the Blue Bar after everyone else had left, they each had one more for the hell of it. Papashvilly had finally said quietly:

"You know what it is?"

"Perhaps."

Papashvilly had smiled to himself. "The world is full of them. And I will tell you something: they have always known they will be left behind. That's why they're so careless and surly."

"Ah."

"The city people and the farmers. They have always known their part in the intent of history. That's why they have their roofs and thick walls—so they can hide and also say that it's no longer out there."

"I wouldn't know what you're talking about. I have no understanding of history."

Papashvilly burst into laughter. At the end of the room, Eddie had looked up briefly from the glass he was toweling. "You know. Some do not. But you know." He smiled and shook his head, drumming impatiently on the edge of their table. "These have been peculiar centuries lately. Look how it was. From the beginning of time, the six-legged came from the steppes, and only the mountains and the seas held some of them away, but not always and not forever.

"For uncounted centuries before the birth of our Christ, they came again and again. Some remained at the edges of the sea, in their cities, and ventured out then beyond the

194

walls to make orchards and plough fields. And again the six-legged would come, and take the cities, and leave their seed, or stay behind and become the city people, to be taken by the next six-legged who came not from the edge of the world—no, we say that in the books, but we mean the center of the world; the *source* of the world. The city people had time for books. The city people are obsessed with making permanent things, because they know they are doomed. The six-legged know something else. They laugh at what you say is the story and the purpose of the world. And the more earnest of manner you are, the more amusing it is, because you know, really, it is all nonsense that you tell yourselves to be more comfortable. You know what the six-legged are. When you were pushed over the edge of the western ocean from your little handhold on what was left to you of Europe, you knew better than to let the six-legged remain free on your prairies, just as we Osseti knew who must not be allowed in the high pastures.

"And so you city people of the west took for yourselves not only the edges beyond the mountains, where you have always had your places for ships and warehouses, but like Ivan you took the great central steppes, too, for a while in which you could build great things.

"Great things. Great establishments on which we all choke, and in which we sit and say the grass is gone forever. It makes us neither honestly happy nor sad to say that; it makes us insane. There are walls, walls, all around us, and no honest tang of the wind and the seed of the grass. We say the walls make us safe, but we fear they make us blind. We say the roof makes us warm, but we know we lie when we pretend there are no stars. I do not, in fact, understand how it is we are not all dead. Ever since Ivan, it has been inevitable we would turn the cannon on ourselves someday. It is not only a great solver of problems, it is pleasurable to see such a mighty end to lies. And yet somehow, when we should close these four so-called civilized centuries in one last pang, we merely bicker and shuffle among ourselves, and tell the lie that we are all more like brothers each day.

"I am a good boy. I have been to Muscovy and not been entirely despised by my masters in our democratic association of freely federated republics. I am friends with Slavs, with Khazaks, with Tartars, and with Turkmen. I am a civilized man, furthermore a crew commander and a fleet commander, and a doctor of engineering. When we go toward mighty Jupiter and approach his great face, when we send in the modules to slice away a little here, and probe out a little there, and suck in a fraction here and there, I shall read all the checklists at the proper time, and all my personnel and I will follow all the manuals exactly. Then the mining extractors will come in a few years, and the orbital factories, and Jupiter shall be garlanded by them. The robotized containers shall flow Earthward; there will be great changes when it is no longer necessary to rip at our soil and burrow ever deeper in our planet, and make stenches and foul the sight of heaven. This much I owe the city people and that part of my blood which comes from men who held on. And, besides, perhaps the grass will come back, and that would be to the liking of those who still live with horses. Who knows?

"I am a good boy. But I see. I see that it was perhaps needful that there be four centuries in which the six-legged were required to bide. I also see that the time is at an end. The establishments have done their work. I would not have believed it; I would say that city ways should have killed us

196

all by now. There are so many machines that must lie for everyone's comfort. But—" He shrugged. "Machines go wrong. With so many, perhaps there is one, somewhere, that does us good, almost by accident, and so blunts the edge of destiny.

"But, you know, I would not risk it much longer." He smiled. "We are already going very far. Next time, we will reach distances such that the radio takes an impossible time to transmit the reports and instructions, is it not so? And the trip is so long. It becomes senseless to return all the way, or to think that someone at a microphone in Africa can control what needs to be done at Neptune, or perhaps at Alpha Centauri. Control, or even advise. No, I think it becomes very natural then to make camps out there, and to have repair depots and such, so that it is not necessary to go to the constant expense and time to go back and forth to here. If we can make food from petroleum and cloth from stone in Antarctica, I think we can find minerals and hydrocarbons in space as well, no?

"I think then we come back once in a while if it is still here; we will come back for new recordings of *Les Sylphides*, and we shall pay for them with gems snatched from the temples of Plutonian fire-lizards, say, or with nearly frictionless bearings, or with research data. We shall tell the Earthmen how the universe is made, and they shall tell romantic stories about us and wish they had time to leave home." Papashvilly shook his head. "Clinging is a thing a man can take pride in, I think, and there is nothing to be ashamed in it. Nothing, especially if one clings so well that nothing can dislodge him. Nevertheless, I have stood on Mount Elbrus and looked northeast, Lavrenti, and from there I could only see as far as one of Timur's hazarras could ride in a week. And I said to myself: I, too, am six-legged." He had put down his empty glass. "Goodbye, alcohol," he had said. A few polite words more and it was time to go. Papashvilly had put his hands on Michaelmas's arms and shaken him a little, fondly. "We shall see each other again," he had said, and had gone up to his room.

Domino said: "The European Flight Authority has determined the cause of Watson's crash."

Michaelmas sat up. They were coming out of the hills, now, and whirling down the flats, leaving a plume of finely divided dust along the shoulder of the highway. "What was it?"

"Desiccator failure."

"Give me some detail."

"The most efficient engine working fluid is, unfortunately, also extremely hygroscopic. It's practically impossible to store or handle it for any length of time without its becoming contaminated with water absorbed from the air.

"The usual methods, however, ensure that this contamination will stay at tolerable levels, and engines are designed to cope with a certain amount of steam mixed into the other vapors at the high-pressure stages. Clear so far? All right; this particular series of helicopter utilizes an engine originally designed for automobiles produced by the same manufacturing combine. The helicopter cabins have the same basic frame as the passenger pod and engine mount of the automobile, the same doors and seats, and share quite a bit of incidental hardware. This series of helicopter can therefore be sold for markedly less than equally capable competing machines, and is thus extremely popular worldwide among corporate fleet buyers. The safety record of the model

Watson was flying is good, and indicates no persistent characteristic defect. However, this is not true of an earlier model, which showed something of a tendency to blockage in its condenser coils. They froze now and then, usually at high altitudes, causing a stoppage of working fluid circulation, and consequent pressure drop followed by an emergency landing or a crash due to power loss."

"Power loss," Michaelmas said. "Like Watson."

"But not quite for the same reason. This is a more recent model, remember. In the earlier ones, it had been found that the downdraft from the helicopter rotors, under certain conditions of temperature and humidity, was creating cold spots in the coils, and causing plugs of ice. This was not a defect in the engine as an automobile engine. So, since it was economically impractical to redesign or to relocate the engine, the choice was between thermostatically heating the coils to one degree Celsius, or in making sure there was never any water in the working fluid passing through the coils.

"Option One resulted in performance losses, and was therefore not acceptable; one reason the helicopter application worked so well was the steep temperature gradient across the coil. So they went to the other choice; they installed a desiccator. This is essentially a high-speed precipitator; exhausted vapor from the high-pressure stages passes through it enroute to the coil. The water vapor component is picked off and diverted below one hundred degrees Celsius into a separate reservoir, where it is electrically superheated back to about one hundred twenty degrees and vented into the atmosphere as chemically pure steam. The electrical load is small, the vent is parallel to the helicopter's long axis so that some of the energy is recovered as an increment of forward motion, and the whole thing has the sort of simplicity that appeals."

"But the unit failed in this case," Michaelmas said.

"It has happened only twice before, and never over Alpine terrain in gusty wind conditions. These were its first two fatalities. What happens if the electrical heating fails is that the extracted moisture vents as water rather than steam, gradually forming a cap of ice, which then creates a backup in the desiccator. The physics of it all then interact with the engineering to rupture the final stage of the desiccator, and this creates a large hole in the plumbing. All the high-pressure vapor vents out through it, in preference to entering the condenser, and half a cycle later the turbine has nothing to work with. Result, power loss; furthermore, the percentage of water required to have it happen is much less than is needed to create condenser freeze-up. You can be almost sure that any charge of working fluid, even a fresh one right out of a sealed flask, will have picked up enough."

"A very dangerous design."

"Most add-on new parts have to compromise-fit the basic hardware, and have to add as little as possible to total unit cost, since they inevitably skew the original profit projections. But as it happens this is a rather good design. The electricity comes from a magneto, gear-driven by the output shaft. The wiring, which you would expect to be the weak spot, is vibration-proofed, and uses astronautics-grade insulation and fasteners. It is also located so that no other part can rub through it, and is routed away from all routine service hatches so that fuel-loaders, fluid-handlers, and other non-mechanics servicing the vehicle cannot accidentally damage the unit. The desiccator has its own inspection hatch, and only certified mechanics are shown how to operate the type of latch used."

They were clearly targeted on Control Tower now; staring forward with his eyes half-focused, Michaelmas could see the structure larger than any of the others, dead ahead, and apparently widening out to either side of the tapering white thread of highway. He glanced back through the rear window; they were being followed by a short caravan of trucks. The lead unit, a white, ground-hugging Oskar with shooting platforms collapsed against its sides like extra accumulators, carried the sunburst insignia of Mr. Samir's crew.

"Then what happened?"

"The European Flight Authority found one wire hanging."

Michaelmas nodded to himself, then grinned humorlessly and looked around for a moment. Everyone was busy doing something or nothing. "What did they think of that?"

"They're not sure. The connection is made with a device called a Pozipfastner; it snaps on, never opens of itself, and nominally requires a special tool for removal."

"Nominally?"

"The fastener sells because it's obviously tamperproof; any purchasing agent can demonstrate to his supervisor that the connection can't break, can't shake loose, and can't be taken apart with a screwdriver or a knife blade. The special removal tool has two opposed spring-loaded fingerlets that apply a precise amount of pressure to two specific points. It's an aerospace development. But any mechanic with any experience at all can open any Pozipfastner by flicking it with his index fingernails. It's a trick that takes almost no practice, and most of them do it; it's much quicker than using the tool."

201

"And I presume anyone on any aircraft service crew knows how to work the special latches that only certified mechanics understand."

"Of course. How could anything get done on time if the nearest man couldn't lend a hand?"

Michaelmas pursed his lips. "What do you make of that wire?"

"Sabotage. The AEV really thinks so too, but they can't bring themselves to accept the idea. Nevertheless, the unit flew without incident early this morning from a charter service to meet Watson. It was parked while Watson held a meeting with his network's local people, but it certainly wasn't serviced during that time. While Watson was talking, someone deliberately opened that hatch and then either used the factory tool or did the fingernail trick. I suppose it might have been someone demonstrating knowledgeability to an acquaintance. I suppose that someone might have forgotten to resnap the connection before remembering to close the hatch all nice and tidy. There might be some reason why such a person chose to demonstrate on a Pozipfastner that could only be reached by opening an inconveniently located hatch, bypassing scores of others more accessible. The AEV has already drafted an order; henceforth, the desiccator circuit must be wired to an instrument-panel-failure telltale light, or the model's airworthiness certificate will be canceled; all existing members of the type are grounded immediately for inspection of quote potential spontaneous failure endquote and installation of the warning light, and so forth. The manufacturer has already filed an objection, citing unreasonable imposition of added cost, since there are several hours' labor involved, but that's pro forma so they can file a compensation claim against the Common Market authority. *Und so weiter.*"

"What about the police?"

"The AEV is thinking of speaking to them about it."

"Will they?"

"The chief examiner's against it, and he's the man on the spot. Some of the headquarters bureaucrats are a little nervous about what could happen if Interpol ever learns they've concealed evidence. But the examiner's point is that any physical evidence—fingerprints, shreds of coat sleeve, theater ticket stubs, accidentally dropped business cards (I'm quoting him; he's a sarcastic person when questioned in his decisions)—was incinerated in the crash. There's no hope of tracing the saboteur. What they have is a loose wire. And the loose wire is an excuse for circulating an order he's wanted put out ever since a mechanic did leave one hanging last year; if they bring in the cops, the manufacturer will just shrug and legitimately claim again that it's not equipment failure. Furthermore, the pilot and the broadcaster were both voluntarily in dangerous professions; and besides, we can let them at least accomplish one last good thing. So it's better all around."

Michaelmas sucked his teeth.

"They still haven't finally decided," Domino said.

"Yes, they have. Every passing minute makes it less advisable to report it as sabotage. Pretty soon they'd also have to account for the reporting delay, and the thought of that will swing it."

"Well, yes."

"So, how was it done? Did Cikoumas hang around the airport? Of course not. What sanatorium employee? What henchman? Who?"

"I'm working on it. Meanwhile, Daugerd's plane has just landed at Hanrassy's dock. Time there is seven thirty-five AM."

203

Michaelmas glanced at his wrist. Two thirty-five PM.

Frontiere leaned across the aisle. "Ten more minutes, Laurent, and we'll be there." Simultaneously, his telephone sounded. He reached into his jacket, took out the instrument, and inserted the privacy plug in his ear, answering the call with his mouth close to the microphone. Then he recoiled pleasurably. "*Dei grazia,*" he said, put the phone away, and stared at Michaelmas incredulously. "You were exactly correct in your jest," he said. He leaned closer. "The sender looks Russian. The assembly technique is Russian. But our analytical equipment shows that some of the *material* only resembles stock Russian material; the molecular structure is off. Our analytical programs caught it and the ones Norwood used at Limberg's did not. A very sophisticated effort was made to take circuit material and make it *seem* like other circuit material of no greater or lesser practicality. Why would the Russians do that? Why should they?"

Frontiere grinned. "No, someone *is* trying to muddle things up. But we can be rather sure it isn't the Chinese, and if it isn't they or the Russians, then the situation is nowhere near as critical." Frontiere grinned. "It's just some accursed radical group that didn't even kill anybody. We can handle that." He sat up straighter. "We were right to delay." He drummed his fingers on the armrest. "All right. What now?" he said absently, his eyes still shining. "What must be done immediately?"

"Well," Michaelmas said equably, "there is still the problem of forestalling Norwood and Limberg. Steps of some sort must be taken quickly. It would be particularly galling now if one or the other lost patience and blurted out his error in all honesty."

Frontiere grimaced. "Just so."

204

"So I suggest," Michaelmas went on, "that the analytical tests be rerun immediately in your laboratories with Norwood in attendance. In fact, let him do the running. And when he gets the correct result, let him call Limberg with it. It's no disgrace to have been wrong. It's only a minor sin of eagerness not to have waited in the first place to use your lab and your engineering analysis computer programs. It's only natural that your equipment would be subtler and more thorough than anything Norwood and Limberg were able to graft onto Limberg's medical software. And Limberg will understand that until the real culprits are identified, absolute silence about the existence of the sender is the best hope of unearthing them."

Frontiere blinked. "You have a swift mind, Laurent."

"Thank you."

Frontiere frowned slowly at Michaelmas. "There may be difficulty. Norwood may not be entirely willing to accept results different from those he found for himself."

Michaelmas glanced down the aisle. "I think you may find him less sure of himself than he has hitherto appeared. More ready to consider that his faculties might err from time to time."

Frontiere's eyes followed Michaelmas's. Norwood was sitting with one heel hooked on the edge of the seat, his chin resting on his knee. His hands were clasped over his shin. His thumbs absently massaged his calf, while he sat silently looking out the window as if cataloguing the familiar things of his youth while the bus sped in among the outbuildings and the perimeter installations. Frontiere contracted his lower lip and raised an eyebrow. He looked over at Michaelmas. "You are a shrewd observer." He stood up smoothly. "Excuse me. I will go speak to him." He touched

Michaelmas's shoulder. "You are an encouraging person to know," he said.

Michaelmas smiled. When Frontiere was down the aisle, he said: "Well, Domino, congratulations."

"I simply took your hint. Now, the interesting news. I did in fact cause UNAC's analytical apparatus to produce the desired result. A competent molecular physicist examining the readouts will be able to determine exactly with what plausible and fully worthy action group the sender is most likely to have originated. Nevertheless, we are not dealing one hundred percent in deception."

"Oh?"

"Daugerd will never find it simply by looking at holograms. UNAC's programs would never have found it unaided. The difference isn't gross. But it's there; there's something about the electrons. . . ."

"Something about the electrons?"

"It's . . . they're all *right;* I mean, they're in the correct places in the proper number, as far as one can tell, and yet. . . . Well, I ran an analogue; built another sender so to speak, using materials criteria I found stored in the physical data banks of the People's Diligent Electronics Technicum at Dneprodzerzhinsk. And it's different. The two things are out of . . . tune . . . with each other, and they shouldn't be; that damned thing has molecules all through it that say loud and clear it's blood kin to ten thousand others just like it from the Dnieper manufacturing complex. Well, it is, it is, but it's a bastard second cousin masquerading as the legitimate twin."

"Can you give me more detail?"

"I—No. I don't think so."

"Are you saying the sender was produced by some organization on the order of a normal dissident group?"

"No. I don't think so. I don't think— I don't believe there is material exactly like that."

"Ah." Michaelmas sat deeper in his chair. The bus entered the shadow of Control Tower, and the windows lightened. The landscape beyond the shadow became a blaze of white. "Did you feel as you did at the sanatorium?"

"I . . . couldn't say. Probably. Yes. I think so."

The bus was pulling up to a halt among the colonnades and metallized glass of the ground level. People began rising to their feet. Mr. Samir, Michaelmas noted through his window, had gotten the Oskar in through the portal and was parking nearby; the sides of the little van metamorphosed into an array of platforms, and a technician was out of the truck and up on the topmost one instantly, slipping one camera into its mount, and reaching down to take another being handed up to him. "What about Norwood?" Michaelmas asked. "When you touched him."

"Norwood? Nor—? No, I wasn't getting anything through the sensors in that terminal. You wouldn't find it with sensors: you have to be electron-to-electron with it. . . . Norwood? What an interesting question! No—there's no way. There's no interface, you see. There's only data. No, I could only feel that with something approximating my own kind."

"Approximating. Yes."

Michaelmas was watching Norwood in conversation with Frontiere. Frontiere was talking intently and softly, holding one hand on Norwood's shoulder and tapping lightly on Norwood's chest with the spread fingers of the other. Norwood was looking into his face with the half-focused stare of an earthquake victim. It was over in a moment. Norwood shrugged and nodded, his eyes downcast. Frontiere smiled and put his arm protectively around Norwood's shoulders in good-natured bonhommie. He patted Norwood's shoulder absently while looking about him for aides to make sure the astronaut's entrance into Control Tower would be properly handled.

"An interesting statement. But hardly relevant at this moment," Michaelmas said. "Your sensors *were* adequate to measure his belief in himself."

"As any other lie detector would have."

"That may be as much detection as any man needs. Well— we're off." The bus was emptying. To keep in trim, Michaelmas stepped forward deftly and debarked just behind Norwood and Frontiere. Not only Ossip Sakal but Hjalmar Wirkola himself were waiting to greet Norwood, all smiles now. There was a faint flicker through the lobby lights, unnoticed. Frontiere propelled the astronaut gently toward the Director General. The stately, straight-backed old gentleman stepped forward from Sakal's side as Norwood approached, and extended his hand. Somewhere very faintly there was a ringing bell, if you listened. "My boy!" Wirkola said, clasping the astronaut's handshake between his palms. "I was so glad when Ossip told me you are all safe now." Everyone's attention was on them. Over at the elevator bank, a security man was looking at the lights of an indicator panel and frowning, his ear to the wall, but that was the sum total of distraction in that crowd.

The press of people built up around Norwood and Wirkola; Michaelmas could see additional UNAC people coming from a side foyer. Getulio's press aides were bringing them in through the more casual onlookers and the news people. There is a lot you can do with a properly swung hip and a strategically insinuated shoulder to create lanes in a crowd without it showing on camera.

There was, somewhere, away in the higher levels of the tower, a dull thump. Perhaps, really, it was a sonic boom outside, somehow penetrating the building insulation. Or masked burglars blowing a safe with black powder. A freight elevator door opened and Papashvilly stepped out, looking momentarily flustered but recovering quickly.

Domino was making the noise again. He had learned to make it clearly, now. It was a bronchitic giggle, brought up sawing from the depths of a chest in desperate search of air. "The building systems program!" he gasped. "It's trying to maintain homeostasis with everything going to hell upstairs. It's running from switch to switch like an old maid chasing mice with a broom. Oh, my! Oh, me!"

Papashvilly had his head up, his shoulders back, and his grin delighted as he moved toward the main group. He was waving at Norwood. As his glance reached Michaelmas, who was making his way across Luis's line of sight on Norwood, he momentarily shifted the direction of his wave, and wagged two fingers at him, before redirecting himself to the welcome. Michaelmas raised a clenched fist, one thumb up, and shook it. Clementine Gervaise stepped on Michaelmas's foot. *"Pardon,"* she said, the corners of her mouth quivering slightly and her eyes a little wider and shining more than normal, "you are blocking my camera, Laurent." Michaelmas stared at her. "Excuse me," he said, wondering if they would now spend days grinning at each other. "It was innocent, I assure you," he said and pushed on, his eyes sliding off Campion's face enroute. The man was looking around a little busily, his face raised. He made a sniffing expression. There was the faintest whiff of smoke in the air, already being dissipated by the building's exhaust ventilators. Campion shrugged faintly and returned his attention to matters at hand. Michaelmas found it interesting that Douggie did have a nose for news. He winked toward Papashvilly.

"Hanrassy is punching up Gately's number," Domino said.

Michaelmas stopped, changed direction, and began working his way clear. "I'll want to monitor that," he said, and pulled the plug out of the terminal, inserting it in his ear as he went, to account for the fact that he was stepping out of the crowd and standing with an intent expression, his hand over his free ear to shut out other sounds. He stood apparently oblivious, while Gately's secretary fielded the call and then put Hanrassy through.

"I want you to look at something, Mr. Secretary," she said without preamble.

Domino said: "She's showing him a holo of the sender."

"Yes," Michaelmas said. He clenched his jaw.

"I see it, Miz Hanrassy. Should I recognize it?" Gately said.

"That would depend on how familiar you expect to be with Soviet electronic devices."

"I don't follow you, ma'am. Is that thing Russian?"

"It is, Mr. Secretary. There's no doubt about it; it's not exactly a standard component in their engineering, but it's made of standard pieces and the workmanship is characteristically theirs."

"Yes, ma'am, and in what way is that relevant to my duties?"

"I wonder if you'd care to call Colonel Norwood and ask him if he found it in his capsule just before he was forced to escape."

Michaelmas took a deep breath. "That's it, then," he said to Domino steadily. "There is no further doubt. Limberg and Cikoumas supplied it to her, along with their story. They don't have the slightest sense of restraint or responsibility. They think we are an ant farm."

"Ma'am," Gately was saying, "are you telling me the

210

Russkis sabotaged Norwood's shuttle and you can *prove* it?"

"The sons of bitches," Michaelmas said. "The bastards. Get me to the sanatorium. Right now. And I arrive without warning. Right?"

"Right."

Viola Hanrassy said: "Ask Norwood, Mr. Secretary. Ask him why UNAC hasn't let him say anything about it."

"Ma'am, where'd you get this information?"

"If you obtain corroboration from Norwood, Mr. Secretary, then I'll be glad to discuss details with you. In fact, Will, I'm holding myself in readiness to work very closely with you on this. We may have the joint duty of alerting the American people to their responsibilities and opportunities in the coming election."

Domino said: "I think that may have been an offer of the Vice Presidency."

"Bribes," Michaelmas said. "They always go to bribes when they're not sure they're on top, and coercion when they are. That's all they know. They really don't believe anyone would help them just on their merits. Well, Christ, at least they're our own. How's my ride to Berne?"

"Wait one."

Gately was saying: "I'll place a call to Africa right away and get back to you."

"Thank you, Mr. Secretary."

"And kiss my bum, both of you," Michaelmas muttered as the connection broke. He was looking around with sharp, darting swings of his eyes, his hands raised in front of him and his feet well apart, so that he was leaning forward against his weight.

"Mr. Michaelmas."

"Yes."

"Get to the airport."

"Right."

He strode directly toward Mr. Samir. "How do you do," he said, thrusting his hand forward.

"How do you do, sir," Mr. Samir said, responding with a calloused palm and a dignified smile. "What are my instructions?"

"There has been a change of plans. I would like to be driven back to Cité d'Afrique immediately."

"As you wish." He turned toward his crew, snapped his fingers and gestured. The men began clambering at the sides of the Oskar. "We depart in ninety seconds, Mr. Michaelmas."

"Thank you." He looked around, and found Harry Beloit preparing to hold the door into the interior lobbies. He paced toward him. "Harry," he said in a low voice. "Please accept my apologies and convey them to Getulio, to Pavel, and the rest. There is another story I must cover in person. I'll be patching back to you as soon as I can."

"No problem," Beloit said.

"Thank you very much." He turned away, then stopped, and shook Beloit's hand. "I would like to sit on the edge of your marsh with your family and yourself some day," he said, and went. He waved to Clementine and got into the Oskar beside Mr. Samir. The lowering door interposed tinted glass across her startled expression. She turned to Campion and nudged his arm. They both looked toward the Oskar as it snapped sideward out of its parking groove and oriented on the outer portal. Mr. Samir himself was driving, his shirt-sleeves rolled back from forearms like Indian clubs; the crew, looking curiously forward toward Michaelmas, were still latching down gear and strapping themselves to their seats in the back cargo space.

"I'll call you," Michaelmas pantomimed toward Clementine, holding up his telephone and mock-punching numbers. But what will I call you? he thought, pushing the phone back into his jacket. He waved to Papashvily, who raised his eyebrows. Mr. Samir accelerated. The portal opened, closed behind them and, computer-monitored, stayed obstinately closed when one news crew tried to follow the famous Mr. Michaelmas and learn what he might be after.

Mr. Samir drove hard. The bristling white van hissed wickedly down the highway eastward. "The airport, please, Mr. Samir," Michaelmas said.

"The military gates," Domino said.

"There are no commercial flights to anywhere for some time," Mr. Samir said. "Do you wish a charter?"

"No, Mr. Samir. Charters file flight plans. I will go to the military end of the field, please."

Mr. Samir nodded. "As you wish. We shall probably remember that you asked to be taken to the Hilton."

"That is always a possibility. My thanks."

"I regret that our opportunity to serve has been so limited."

"I will be sending you back to Star Control as soon as you've dropped me. And there will be other times we can work together in person. I anticipate them with pleasure."

"It is mutual."

Domino said: "Gately has a call in for Norwood. They're holding; Norwood should be free in a few minutes. I think UNAC's anticipating a simple message of congratulations from the US administration. They'll put it through quickly."

Michaelmas's mouth thinned into an edged smile. "Good." He watched the desert hurtling past.

"Douglas Campion," Domino said.

213

"Say again."

"While in Chicago at WKMM, Campion was on the crimecopter crew for a year and a half. They flew a model identical to the one in which Watson crashed. They never had any mechanical failures. But the pilot had had a coil freeze-up while flying the earlier model. The station used one until a few months before Campion joined their staff. The pilot put it down in Lincoln Park without further incident, and not much was made of it. But in a year and a half of making conversation five days a week, he probably would have mentioned it to Campion. That could have led to a clinical discussion of causes and cures. I think Campion could have learned how to work latches and Pozipfastners. I think he would know which wire to pull."

Michaelmas bowed his head. "That's pretty circumstantial," he said at last.

"Campion is also on the short list of persons who could have gotten to the machine; Watson was busy talking to his staff, but Campion would already know what he was going to say, and could wander off."

"Being on the list doesn't prove . . ."

"I have attempted to establish corroboration. I found that *National Geographic* had leased facilities on an AP Newsfeatures satellite that was passing over Switzerland at the time. They were using its infrared mapping capabilities for a story on glacial flow. I went through their data and played a few reprocessing tricks with a segment covering Berne. I have identified thermal tracks that correspond to Watson, the helicopter pilot, and several people who must number Campion among them. I have isolated one track as being Campion with eight-two percent certainty. That track leaves

214

the knot of people around Watson, walks around a corner to the helicopter, pauses beside the fuselage at the right place for the proper amount of time, and then rejoins the group." Michaelmas bit his upper lip. He stared straight out through the windshield with his fists in his lap. "Eighty-two percent."

"Eighty-two percent probability that he's the particular member of a restricted group in which only the pilot seems to have been equally qualified to arrange her own death."

Michaelmas said nothing. Then after a while he said: "I hate acting on probability."

"You go to your church and I'll go to mine."

Michaelmas shook his head. Mr. Samir, who doubtless had excellent peripheral vision, appeared to blink once, sharply, but he continued to drive relentlessly.

Oh, yes. Yes. It was as plain as the nose in your mirror. The poor, silly, ambitious son of a bitch had known exactly what would happen. The helicopter would ice up, set down uneventfully in the local equivalent of Lincoln Park, but at some remove from the nearest cab stand, and Douggie Campion instead of Horse Watson would be the main spokesman on worldwide air. Afterward, Horse would be rescued, and it would just have been one of those things.

And how did he salve himself now, assuming he felt the need? That, too, wasn't particularly difficult. He'd understood all the factors, hadn't he? He'd calculated the risk exactly. All right, then, he'd done everything needful; bad luck had killed two people, one of whom happened to be his professional superior, thus creating a permanent vacancy at a higher rung on the ladder; it was funny how Fate worked.

"Keep him busy," Michaelmas growled.

"It's done," Domino said at once.

"Thank you."

"I have Gately's call to Norwood," Domino said as they swept out of the hills and plunged toward the city. "Norwood's in Wirkola's office now."

"Put it on."

"Right."

Michaelmas sat still.

"Walt? Walt, hey, boy, this is Willie!" began in his ear, and continued for some time, during which the expected congratulations and the obligatory God-damns were deployed. Then Gately said: "Listen, son. Can I ask you about something, between the two of us? You got many people looking over your shoulder right this minute?"

"No, not too many, sir. I'm in Mr. Wirkola's office, and there's no one here who isn't UNAC."

"Well, that—forgive me, son, but that may not be—"

"It's okay, Mr. Secretary."

There was a pause. Then Gately made a frustrated, snorting noise. "Okay. What the hell. Have a look—do you recognize this?"

Domino said: "It's his recording of the sender holo."

"Yes, sir, I do," Norwood said. "I'm a little surprised to see you have a picture of it."

"Walter, I've got my sources and I don't mind if UNAC knows that. I'm sure they recognize my right to keep in touch. What about this thing, son? Do you feel you can tell me anything about it over this line at this time?"

"Up to a point, sir. Yes."

"What's that mean?"

There was the sound of a palm being placed over a microphone, and then being lifted off.

216

"Mr. Secretary, have you heard that thing is Russian?"

"That's exactly what I've heard. I've also heard UNAC won't let you say so. How are you today, Mr. Wirkola?"

Norwood said: "Mr. Secretary, I'm looking at a materials analysis printout that says the core component was made by spark-eroding a piece of G.E. Lithoplaque until it looks a lot like U.S.S.R. Grade II Approved stock. You'd think that could work because Grade II is manufactured someplace south of Kiev using equipment purchased from G.E. and utilizing G.E. processes under license. But G.E. went to a smooth from a matte finish on Lithoplaque last year, whereas Grade II didn't. You might figure you could carve back to the old configuration. But you can't; G.E. also changed the structure a little. And it's only in limited distribution as yet. According to what I see here, the only place you could get that particular piece we're talking about is G.E.'s central midwestern supply warehouse in St. Louis."

"St. Louis?"

Mr. Wirkola said: "I am fine. And how are you, Mr. Gately?"

There was a long silence. "You're sure, Walter?"

"Well, to satisfy myself I'm immediately going to pass the thing through the labs here again. I've got to admit I damned near made a fool of myself about it once, and I don't want to do that twice. But we're working with the best hardware and software in the world when it comes to engineering, around here, and I've strapped myself into it many's the time without a second thought. I've got a feeling I could run this baby through any modern equipment in the world and come up with the same answer."

"St. Louis, Missouri."

Mr. Wirkola said: "I believe there is still a community

217

called St. Louis du Ha! Ha!, near Lac Temiscouata in Quebec."

"Mr. Wirkola, I appreciate UNAC's discretion in this matter," Gately said. "I'm assuming you'll be in touch with me officially about this?"

"Yes," Wirkola said. "We are assigning Colonel Norwood to temporary duty as our liaison with the US government on this matter. I suggest a goodwill tour of the USA as a cover for his talks with your President and yourself. But he will call you a little later today with confirmation from his retests, and that will have given you time to consult with Mr. Westrum on your response to that suggestion. You may tell Mr. Westrum we understand his political situation, and we certainly do not wish to inculcate any unnecessary constraints upon his conscience. Nevertheless, I think there may be better ways to slide this incident into the back shelves of history than by any public counterclaiming between Mr. Westrum and whoever your informant may have been. What is done privately is of course private."

Domino said: "Slit you, skin you, and sell you a new suit. That nice old man took two minutes to react to Gately's news, size it up, and flip through the anatomy text."

"Yes," Michaelmas said.

"Thank you, Mr. Wirkola," Gately said. "I'll speak to my President and be waiting for Colonel Norwood's call."

"Thank you, Mr. Secretary. We are grateful for your cooperation," Wirkola said.

"Bye, Walter. Good to talk to you, son."

"Thank you, Mr. Secretary."

The connection opened. The van was on the city ramps now, sliding smoothly between the beautiful new structures, humming toward the airport. Domino said: "I can see why you favored Mr. Wirkola's election as Director General."

"That's not what you see. What you see is why it wasn't necessary to do anything with the vote. His virtues are evident even to an election committee. Eschew the sin of overmanagement; that above all. You don't want to lose respect for the Hjalmar Wirkolas of this world."

"Noted. As before."

Michaelmas sighed. "I didn't mean to nag."

He made his voice audible: "Mr. Samir, after you've delivered me, I'd like you to go back to Star Control and interview Major Papashvilly. Permission's all arranged. After I'm airborne, I'll call Signor Frontiere and the Major, and tell them you're coming and what we'll do."

"Right," Domino said.

"I understand," Mr. Samir replied.

Michaelmas smiled trustfully at him. "You have it. I'll be on the phone with you, giving you the questions to ask, and you'll pick up the Major's responses."

"No problem," Domino said.

"I understand completely," Mr. Samir said. "I am proud of your reliance on me."

"Then there's no difficulty," Michaelmas said. "Thank you."

Mr. Samir's footage would be fed to his network's editing storage and held for mixing. Via Domino, the network would also receive footage of Michaelmas asking the questions, commenting, and reacting to Papashvilly's answers. The network editing computer would then mix a complete interview out of the two components.

Since the shots of Michaelmas would be against a neutral background, the editing program could in some cases scale Michaelmas and Papashvilly into conformity and matte them into the same frames together. The finished effect would be quite convincing. Mr. Samir assumed, without the impolite-

219

ness of asking, that Michaelmas would also use a union crew at his end.

And in fact he would, Michaelmas thought as he leaned back in his seat. Domino would call in direct to network headquarters, and they'd photo the Laurent Michaelmas hologram in their own studios. You could do that with studio-controlled lighting and computer-monitored phone input levels. There was a promise that only a year or two from now there'd be equipment that would let you do it in the field. When that happened, it wouldn't be necessary any longer for L. G. Michaelmas to be physically present anywhere but in his apartment, sitting at his desk or cooking in his kitchen or playing his upside-down-strung guitar.

"What'll you want?" Domino asked. "A how's-it-going-Pavel, or a give-us-the-big-picture, or a roundup conversation including how he reacts to Norwood's return or what?"

"Give us the roundup," Michaelmas said. "He'll be good at that. We just want to reinforce the idea he's a bright, quick, fine fellow and he's going to do a hell of a job." And mostly, they were simply going to keep Papashvily in a controlled situation among friendly people for the next hour or two. It would do no harm. And it would maintain L. G. Michaelmas's reputation for never scrubbing a job even if he had to be in two places at the same time, damn near, and it was good to remind yourself there were plenty of competent crews and directors around. "And, listen, make sure I'm in character when I phone Pavel about this."

"That's all taken into account. Chat before shooting. Friends reunited. Buy you a drink soonest."

"Fine," Michaelmas said. He rubbed his thumb and fingers over his eyelids, head bowed momentarily, aware that when he slumped like this, he could notice the fatigue in his back and shoulders.

       o   o   o

Something overhead was coming down as if on a string, metallic and glimmering—God's lure. The military gates opened smoothly, so that the Oskar barely slowed. The guard nodded at their plate number and saluted, good soldier, explicit orders fresh in the gate shack teleprinter. The van moved toward the flight line. "What is that?" Mr. Samir asked, looking up and out through the windscreen. He braked hard and stopped them at the edge of a hardstand.

The aircraft became recognizable overhead as a cruelly angled silvery wedge balanced on its tailpipes, but as it neared the ground its flanks began to open into stabilizer surfaces, landing struts, and blast deflectors.

"I believe that is a Type Beta Peacekeeper," Michaelmas said. "They are operated by the Norwegian Air Militia. I wouldn't open any doors or windows until it's down and the engines are idled." The windscreen glass began shivering in its gaskets, and the metal fabric of the Oskar began to drum.

Domino said: "It's on a routine checkride to Kirkenes from the base at Cap Norvegia in the Antarctic. It's now had additions to the mission profile for purposes of further crew training. What you see is an equatorial sea-level touchdown; another has been changed in for the continental mountains near Berne. Excellent practice. Meantime, one unidentified passenger will be aboard on priority request from the local embassy which, like many another, occasionally does things that receive no explanation and whose existence is denied and unrecorded. Hardstand contact here is in thirty seconds; a boarding ladder will deploy. Your programmed flying time is twenty minutes. *Bon voyage.*" The Beta came to rest. The engines quieted into a low rumble that caused little grains of stone to dance an inch above the concrete.

"Goodbye, Mr. Samir. Thank you," Michaelmas said. He

popped open the door and trotted through the blasts of sunlight, hugging the little black box to his ribs. A ladder ramp meant to accommodate an outrushing full riot squad folded down out of the fuselage like a backhand return. He scrambled up it into the load space; a padded, nevertheless thrumming off-green compartment with hydraulically articulated seats that hung empty on this mission. He dropped into one and began pulling straps into place. The ladder swung up and sealed.

"Are you seated and secure, sir?" asked an intercom voice from somewhere beyond the blank upper bulkhead. He sorted through the accent and hasty memories of the language. He snapped the last buckle into place. "Ja," he said, pronouncing the 'a' somewhere nearer 'o' than he might have, and hoping that would do. "Then we're going," said the unseen flight crew member, and the Type Beta first flowed upward and then burst upward. Michaelmas's jaw sagged, and he tilted back deeply against the airbagged cushions. His arms trailed out over the armrests. He said slowly to Domino: "One must always be cautious when one rubs your lamp." But he sat unsmiling, and while there might have been times when he would have been secretly delighted with the silent robotics of the seat suspensions, which kept him ever facing the direction of acceleration as the Peacekeeper topped out its ballistic curve and prepared to swap ends, he was gnawing at other secrets now. He drummed his fingertips on the cushiony armrest and squirmed. His mouth assumed the expression he kept from himself. "We have a few minutes," he said at last. "Is this compartment secure?"

"Yes, sir."

"I think we might let Douglas Campion find me at this time."

His phone rang. "Hello?" he said.

"What? Who's this? I was calling—" Campion said.

"This is Laurent Michaelmas."

"Larry! Jesus, the damnedest things are happening. How'd I get you? I'm standing here in the UNAC lobby just trying to get through to my network again. Something's really screwed up."

Michaelmas sat back. "What seems to be the trouble, Doug? Is there some way I can help you?"

"Man, I hope somebody can. I—well, hell, you're the first call I've gotten made in this last half hour. Would you believe that? No matter who I call, it's always busy. My network's busy, the cab company's busy. When I tried a test by calling Gervaise from across the room, I got a busy signal. And she wasn't using her phone. Something's crazy."

"It sounds like a malfunction in your instrument."

"Yeah. Yeah, but the same kinds of things happened when I went over and borrowed hers. Look, I don't mean to sound like somebody in an Edgar Allan Poe, but I can't even reach phone Repair Service."

"Good heavens! What will you do if this curse extends?"

"What do you mean?"

"Have you had anyone call you since this happened?"

"No. No—you mean, can anybody reach *me*?"

"Yes, there's that. Then, of course, a natural thing to wonder about is whether your bank is able to receive and honor credit transfers, whether the Treasury Department is continuing to receive and okay your current tax flow.... That sort of thing. Assuming now that you find some way to get back across the ocean, will your building security system recognize you?" He chuckled easily. "Wouldn't that be a pretty pickle? You'd become famous, if anyone could find you."

"My God, Larry, that's not funny."

"Oh, it's not likely to be lifelong, is it? Whatever this thing is? It's just some little glitch somewhere, I should think. Don't you expect it'll clear up?"

"I don't know. I don't know what the hell. Look—where are you, anyway? What made you take off like that? What's going on?"

"Oh, I'm chasing a story. You know what that's like. How do you feel? Do you think it's really serious?"

"Yeah—listen, could you call Repair Service for me? This crazy thing won't let even Gervaise or anybody here do it when I ask them. But if you're off someplace in the city, that ought to be far enough away from whatever this short circuit is or whatever."

"Of course. What's your—" Michaelmas closed his phone and sat again while the aircraft flew. He pictured Campion turning to Gervaise again.

"Mr. Michaelmas," Domino said after some silence. "I just got Konstantinos Cikoumas's export license pulled. Permanently. He might as well leave Africa."

"Very good."

"Hanrassy has placed two calls to Gately in the past ten minutes and been told he was on another line."

"Ah."

"Gately's talking to Westrum."

"Yes."

"When they get confirmation from Norwood, they'll accept Wirkola's plan. Then Westrum will call Hanrassy and play her a recording of Norwood's confirming data. Gately was very pleased that Mr. Westrum was making it unnecessary for Gately to speak to her at all."

"It's funny how things work out."

"You'll be landing in a few moments. Touchdown point is the meadow beyond the sanatorium parking lot. Even so, we may unsettle the patients."

"Can't be helped. If they can stand news crews, they can absorb anything. That's fine, Domino. Thank you."

There was another pause.

"Mr. Michaelmas."

"Yes."

"I'll stay as close as I can. I don't know how near that will be. If any opportunity affords itself, I'll be there."

"I know."

The flight crewman's voice said: "We are coming down now. A bell will ring." The vibration became fuller, and the tone of the engines changed. Michaelmas sank and rose in his cushions, cradling the terminal in his hands. There was a thump. The bell rang and the ladder flew open. Michaelmas hit his quick release, slid out of his straps, and dropped down the ladder. "*Danke,*" he said.

He stepped out into the meadow above the parking lot, looking down at where they'd been parked, and the long steps down which the lens had rolled. He strode quickly forward, quartering across the slope toward the sanatorium entrance. Sanatorium staff were running forward across the grass.

"I have to go," Domino said. "I can feel it again."

"Yes. Listen—it's best to always question yourself. Do you understand the reasons for that?"

There was no reply from the terminal.

The attendants were close enough so that he was being recognized. They slowed to a walk and frowned at him. He smiled and nodded. "A little surprise visit. I must speak to Doctors Limberg and Cikoumas about some things. Where are they? Is it this way? I'll go there." He moved through them toward the double doors, and through the doors. He passed the place where she'd broken her heel. He pushed down the corridor toward the research wing, his mind automatically following the floor plan Harry Beloit had shown Clementine. "Not a public area?" he was saying to some staff person at his elbow. "But I'm not of the public. I speak to the public. I must see Doctors Limberg and Cikoumas." He came to the long cool pastel hallway among the labs. Limberg and Cikoumas were coming out of adjoining hall doors, staring at him, as the Type Beta rumbled up. "Ah, there!" he said, advancing on them, spreading his arms and putting his hands on their shoulders. "Exactly so!" he exclaimed with pleasure. "Exactly the people I want. We have to talk. Yes. We have to talk." He turned them and propelled them toward Limberg's door. "Is this your office, Doctor? Can we talk in here? It seems comfortable enough. We need privacy. Thank you, Doctors. Yes." He closed the door behind him, chatty and beaming. "Well, now!" He propped one buttock on the corner of Limberg's desk. The two of them were standing in the middle of the floor, looking at him. He was counting in his head. He estimated about thirty minutes since Norwood's conversation with Gately. "Well, here we three are!" he said, resting his hands on his thighs and leaning toward them attentively. "Yes. Let's talk."

Twelve

Limberg put his head back and looked at him warily, his lips pursing. Then his mouth twitched into a flat little grimace. He turned and dropped into one of the two very comfortable-looking stuffed chairs. Against the raspberry-colored velour, he seemed very white in his crisp smock and his old skin and hair. He brought his knees together and sat with his hands lying atop them. He cocked his head and said nothing. His eyes darted sideward toward Cikoumas, who was just at the point of drawing himself up rigid and thrusting his hands into his pockets. Cikoumas said: "Mister—ah—Michaelmas—"

"Larry. Please; this isn't a formal interview."

"This is no sort of interview at all," Cikoumas said, his composure beginning to return. "You are not welcome here; you are not—"

227

Michaelmas raised an eyebrow and looked toward Limberg. "I am not? Let me understand this, now . . . Medlimb Associates is refusing me hospitality before it even knows the subject I propose, and is throwing me out the door summarily?" He moved his hand down to touch the comm unit hanging at his side.

Limberg sighed softly. "No, that would be an incorrect impression." He shook his head slightly. "Dr. Cikoumas fully understands the value of good media relations." He glanced at Cikoumas. "Calm yourself, Kristiades, I suggest to you," he went on in the same judicious voice. "But, Mr. Michaelmas, I do not find your behavior unexceptionable. Surely there is such a thing as calling for an appointment?"

Michaelmas looked around him at the office with its rubbed shelves of books, its tapestries and gauzy curtains, its Bokhara carpet and a broad window gazing imperviously out upon the slopes and crags of a colder, harsher place. "Am I interrupting something?" he asked. "It seems so serene here." How much longer can it take to run? he was asking himself, and at the same time he was looking at Cikoumas and judging the shape of that mouth, the dexterity of those hands which quivered with ambition. "It's only a few questions, Kiki," he said. "That's what they call you, isn't it—Kiki?"

Cikoumas suddenly cawed a harsh, brief laugh. "No, Mr. Michaelmas, *they* don't call me Kiki," he said knowingly. "Is that what you're here to ask?"

"Would he have found some way to beg a lift on a military aircraft," Limberg commented, "if that was the gravity of his errand?"

It didn't seem Cikoumas had thought that through. He frowned at Michaelmas now in a different way, and held himself more tensely.

228

Michaelmas traced a meaningless pattern on the rug with his shoe-tip. He flicked a little dust from his trouser leg, extending his wristwatch clear of his cuff. "A great many people owe me favors," he said. "It's only fair to collect, once in a while."

There was a chime in the air. "Dr. Limberg," a secretarial voice said. "You have an urgent telephone call." Michaelmas looked around with a pleasant, distracted smile.

"I cannot take it now, Liselotte," Limberg said. "Ask them to call later."

"It may be from Africa," Michaelmas said.

Cikoumas blinked. "I'll see if they'll speak to me. I'll take it in my office." He slipped at once through the connecting door at the opposite side of Limberg's desk. Michaelmas traded glances with Limberg, who was motionless. "Liselotte," Limberg said, "is it from Africa?"

"Yes, *Herr Doktor.* Colonel Norwood. I am giving the call to Dr. Cikoumas now."

"Thank you." Limberg looked closely at Michaelmas. "What has happened?" he asked carefully.

Michaelmas stood up and strolled across the room toward the window. He lifted the curtain sideward and looked out. "He'll be giving Cikoumas the results of the engineering analysis on the false telemetry sender," he said idly. He scratched his head over his left ear. He swept the curtain off to the side, and turned with the full afternoon light behind him. He leaned his shoulders against the cool plate glass.

Limberg was twisted around in his chair, leaning to look back at him. "I had heard you were an excellent investigative reporter," he said.

"I'd like to think I fill my role in life as successfully as you have yours."

Limberg frowned faintly. A silence came over both of them. Limberg turned away for a moment, avoiding the light upon his eyes. Then he opened his mouth to speak, beginning to turn back, and Michaelmas said: "We should wait for Cikoumas. It will save repeating."

Limberg nodded slowly, faced forward again, and nodded to himself again. Michaelmas stayed comfortably where he was, facing the connecting door. The glass behind him was thrumming slightly, but no one across the room could see he was trembling, and the trembling had to do only with his body. Machinery hummed somewhere like an elevator rising, and then stopped.

Cikoumas came back after a few moments. He peered at Michaelmas up the length of the room. Behind him there was a glimpse of white angular objects, a gleam of burnished metals, cool, even lighting, a pastel blue composition tile floor. Then he closed the door. "There you are." He progressed to a show of indignation. "I have something confidential to discuss with Dr. Limberg."

"Yes," Michaelmas said. "About the telemetry sender." Cikoumas made his face blank.

Limberg turned now. "Ah." He raised a hand sideward. "Hush one moment, Kristiades. Mr. Michaelmas, can you tell us something about the sender?"

Michaelmas smiled at Cikoumas. "Norwood has told you UNAC's analytical computer programs say the sender isn't Russian. It's a clever fake." He smiled at Limberg. "He says it's probably from Viola Hanrassy's organization."

Cikoumas and Limberg found themselves trying to exchange swift glances. Limberg finally said: "Mr. Michaelmas, why would they think it's from Hanrassy?"

230

"When it isn't? Are you asking how has UNAC fooled Norwood?"

Cikoumas twitched a corner of his mouth. "To do that, as you may not realize, they would have to reprogram their laboratory equipment. Events have been too quick for them to do that."

"Ah. Well, then, are you asking why has Norwood become a liar, when he left here so sincere?"

Limberg shook his head patiently. "He is too fine a man for that." His eyes glittered briefly. "Please, Mr. Michaelmas. Explain for me." He waved silence toward Cikoumas again. "I am old. And busy."

"Yes." Not as busy as some. "Well, now, as to why the sender appears a fake, when we all know it should appear genuine...." He rubbed his knuckles gently in his palm. "Sincere. If it could talk; if there was a way you could ask it Did He who made the lamb make Thee, it would in perfect honesty say *Da*." And how does it do that, I wonder. Or how did they convince it? Which is it? What's that noise beyond Cikoumas's door? "Then if you see the impossible occurring, Doctors, I would say perhaps there might be forces on this Earth which you had no way of taking into account." He addressed himself directly to Limberg. "It's not your fault, you see?"

Limberg nodded. The flesh around his mouth folded like paper.

Cikoumas dropped his jaw. "How much *do* you know?"

Michaelmas smiled and spread his palms. "I know there's a sincere Walter Norwood, where once over the Mediterranean there was nothing. Nothing," he said. "He'll be all right; nice job in the space program, somewhere. Administrative. Off flight status; too many ifs. Grow older. Cycle out, in time. Maybe get a job doing science commentary for some network." Michaelmas straightened his shoulders and stood away from the window. "It's all come apart, and you can't repeat it, you can't patch it up. Your pawns are taken. The Outer Planets expedition will go, on schedule, and others will follow it." And this new sound, now.

It was a faint ripple of pure tones, followed by a mechanical friction as something shifted, clicked, and sang in one high note before quieting. Perhaps they didn't know how acute his ear for music was. Cikoumas had taken longer in there than he might have needed for a phone call.

Limberg said: "Mr. Michaelmas—these unknown forces . . . you are in some way representative of them?"

"Yes," Michaelmas said, stepping forward. His knees were stiff, his feet arched. "I am they." His mouth stretched flat and the white ridges of his teeth showed. The sharp breath whistled through them as he exhaled the word. "Yes." He walked toward Cikoumas. "And I think it's time you told your masters that I am at their gates." As if I were deaf and they were blind. He stopped one step short of Cikoumas, his face upturned to look directly at the man. There's something in there. In his eyes. And in that room.

Cikoumas smiled coldly. That came more naturally to him than the attempts to act indecision or fear. "The opportunity is yours, Mr. Michaelmas," he said, bowing from the waist a little and turning to open the door. "Please follow me. I must be present to operate the equipment at the interview."

"Kristiades," Limberg said softly from his chair, "be wary of him."

There was no one beyond the door when Michaelmas followed Cikoumas through it.

232

It was a white and metal room of moderate size, its exterior wall paneled from floor to ceiling with semiglobular plastic bays, some translucent and others transparent, so that the mountains were repeated in fish-eye views among apparent circles of milky light. Overhead was the latest in laboratory lighting technique: a pearl-colored fog that left no shadows and no prominences. The walls were in matte white; closed panels covered storage. The composition underfoot was very slightly yielding.

To one side there was a free-standing white cylindrical cabinet, two and a half meters tall, nearly a meter wide. The faintest seams ran vertically and horizontally across its softly reflective surface. It jutted solidly up from the floor, as though it might be a continuation of something below.

Ahead of Michaelmas were storage cubes, work surfaces, instrumentation panels, sterile racks of teasing needles, forceps and scalpels, microtomes, a bank of micromanipulative devices—all shrouded beneath transparent flexible dust hoods or safe behind glassy panels.

Michaelmas looked around further. At his other hand was the partition wall to Limberg's office. From chest height onward, it was divided into small white open compartments like dovecotes. Below that was a bare workshelf and a tall, pale-blue-upholstered laboratory stool to sit on. Cikoumas motioned toward it. "Please."

Michaelmas raised his eyebrows. "Are we waiting here to meet someone?"

Cikoumas produced his short laugh. "It cannot come in here. It doesn't know where we are. Even if it did, it couldn't exist unprotected here." He gestured to the chair again. "Please." He reached into one of the pigeonholes and produced a pair of headphones at the end of a spiral cord. "I do not like the risk of having this voice overheard," he said.

233

"Listen." He cupped one earpiece in each hand and moved toward Michaelmas. "You want to know?" he said, twisting his mouth. "Here is knowledge. See what you make of it."

Michaelmas grunted. "And what would you like to know?"

Cikoumas shrugged. "Enough to decide whether we must surrender to these forces of yours or can safely dispose of you, of course."

Michaelmas chuckled once. "Fair enough," he said, and sat down. His eyes glittered hard as he watched Cikoumas's hands approach his skull. "Lower away."

Cikoumas rested the headphones lightly over his ears. Then he reached up and pulled out another set for himself. He stood close by, his hands holding each other, bending his body forward a little as if to hear better.

The voice was faint, though strong enough, probably, at its origins, but filtered, attenuated, distant, hollow, cold, dank: "Michaelmasss . . ." it said. "Is that you? Cikoumas tells me that is you. Isss that what you are—Michaelmasss?"

Michaelmas grimaced and rubbed the back of his neck. "How do I answer it?" he asked Cikoumas, who momentarily lifted one earpiece.

"Speak," Cikoumas said, shifting eagerly around him. "You are heard."

"This is Michaelmas."

"An entity . . . you consider yourself an intelligent entity."

"Yes."

"Distinguishable in some manner from Limberg and Cikoumasss. . . ."

"Yes."

"What does A equal?"

"Pi R squared."

234

"What is the highest color of rainbows?"

"Red."

"Would you eat one of your limbs if you were starving?"

"Yes."

"Would you eat Cikoumas or Limberg if you were starving?"

Cikoumas was grinning faintly at him.

"First," Michaelmas said coldly.

"An entity ... to speak to an intelligent entity ... in these circumstances of remoteness and displacement ... you have no idea how it feels ... to have established contact with three entities, now, under these peculiar circumstances ... to take converse with information-processors totally foreign ... never of one's accustomed bone and blood...."

"I—ah—have some idea."

"You argue?"

"I propose."

"Marriage?"

"No. Another form of dialectical antagonism."

"We are enemiesss ... ? You will not join with Limberg and Cikoumas ... ?"

"Why should I? What will you give?"

"I will make you rich and famous among your own ... kind.... Contact with my skills can be translated into rewards which are somehow gratifying to you ... individuals.... Cikoumas and Limberg can show you how it'sss done...."

"No."

"Repeat. Clarify. Synonimize."

"Negative. Irrevocable refusal. Contradiction. Absolute opposition. I will not be one of your limbs." He grinned at Cikoumas.

235

"Ah-hah! Ah-hah! Ah-hah! Then is your curiosity in the name of what you think science. . . ?"

"Justice."

"Ah-hah! Ah-hah! Complex motivations. . . ! Ah-hah! The academician Zusykses sssaid to me this would be so; he said the concept is not of existences less than ours, but apart from oursss in origin only, reflecting perfectly that quality which we define as the high faculties; I am excited by your replies. . . . I shall tell my friend, Zusykses, when we reunite with each other this afternoon; his essential worth is validated!"

"I might be lying."

"We know nothing of lies. . . . No, no, no . . . in the universe, there is this and there is that. This is not that. To say this is that is to hold up to ridicule the universe. And that is an absurd proposition."

"What is it, then, that isn't the truth but isn't a lie?"

Cikoumas looked at him with sudden intensity. But Michaelmas was nearly blind with concentration.

"Shrewd . . . you are a shrewd questioner . . . you speak of probability . . . yesss . . . it was my darling Zusykses who proposed the probability models of entities like you; who declared this structure was possible, and ssso must exist somewhere because the universe is infinite, and in infinity all things must occur. And yet this is only a philosophical concept, I said in rebuttal. But let me demonstrate, said my preceptor, Zusykses, in ardor to me; here, subordinate academician Fermierla, take here this probability coherence device constructed in accordance with my postulates . . . while away this noon and ssseek such creaturesss as I say must be, for you shall surely find their substance somewhere flung within Creation's broadly scattered arms; take them up, meld

236

of their varied strains that semblance which can speak and touch in simulacrum of a trueborn soul; regard then visage, form and even claim of self. Return to me, convinced—we tremble at the brink of learning all that life is. Clasp to yourself my thought made manifest, which is my self; know it, accept it, make it one with us; I shall not sssend you from me anymore...."

Michaelmas looked at Cikoumas, frowning. He lifted off the headphones but held them near his ears. Fermierla's voice continued faintly.

"It thinks we are chance occurrences," Cikoumas said drily. "It says this Zusykses, whatever it is, deduced that humanity must exist, since its occurrence is possible within the natural laws of the infinite universe. The probability of actually locating it to prove him right is, of course, infinitely small. So they think they are communicating with a demonstration model. Something they created with this probability coherer of theirs. It isn't likely to them that this is the human world. It's likelier that accidental concentrations of matter, anywhere in the universe, are moving and combining in such a manner that, by pure chance, they perfectly match infinitesimal portions of Zusykses' concept. Zusykses and Fermierla think the coherer detects and tunes an infinitely large number of these infinitely small concentrations together into an intelligible appearance. They think we might actually be anything—a sort of Brownian movement in the fabric of the universe—but that entirely at random in an infinity of chances, these selected particles invariably act to present the appearance of intelligent creatures in a coherent physical system."

"Just one?" Michaelmas asked sharply.

Cikoumas's head twitched on its long, thin neck. "Eh?"

"You're talking as if ours is the only probability Fermierla can reach with the coherer. But why should that be? He has his choice of an infinity of accidentally replicated pseudohuman environments, complete with all our rocks and trees and Boy Scout knives. It's all infinite, isn't it? Everything has to happen, and nearly everything has to happen, and everything twice removed, and thrice, and so forth?"

Cikoumas licked his lips. "Oh. Yes. I suppose so. It seems a difficult concept. I must be quite anthropomorphic. And yet I suppose at this moment an infinite number of near-Fermierlas are saying an infinitely varied number of things to an infinity of us. A charming conceit. Do you know they also have absolutely no interest in where we actually are in relation to each other? Of course, they don't think we actually exist. And incidentally, where they are, this Fermierla creature has been waiting for afternoon since before Dr. Limberg was my age. So there are massive displacements; the gravitic, temporal and electronic resistances involved must be enormous."

"The what?"

"The resistances." Cikoumas gestured impatiently. "The universe is relativistic—You've heard of that, surely?— and although, as a life scientist, I am not concerned with all the little details of non-Newtonian physics, I read as much as I have time for—"

"Good enough, Doctor," Michaelmas said. "There's no point attempting to match your breadth of knowledge and my capacity just now." He put the headphones back over his ears. The skin on his forearms chafed against his shirtsleeves in ten thousand places. Out of the corner of his eye he saw Cikoumas moving casually and reaching up to another pigeonhole.

"...fascinating possibilities ... to actually collaborate in experiments with you ... entities. Zusykses will be beside himself! How fares the astronaut; is it still viable? How does it act? Does it display some sign it is aware it has been tuned from one probability to another ... to reality, pardon."

"He's well enough," Michaelmas replied.

"It was a waste," Cikoumas said distractedly. He was manipulating some new control up there, both hands hidden to the wrists while he turned his head to look over Michaelmas's shoulder. But he was trying to watch Michaelmas at the same time.

"Ah, that'sss a shame! You had such hopes for it a little while ago, Cikoumas! Perhaps then we should be obtaining the second Michaelmas from not that same probability.... What's your opinion, gentlemen?"

Michaelmas was on his feet, facing Cikoumas, the flexcord stretching nearly to its limit as he turned. Something had begun to whine and sing behind him. Cikoumas stared into his eyes, in the act of pulling one hand away from the wall, the custom-checkered walnut grip of a pistol showing at the bulge of reddish white palm and bony thumb. Michaelmas tore off the headphones and threw them at him. The strap for Domino's terminal, hung over his left shoulder, dropped across his forearm, twisted, and caught firmly there below his elbow. Spinning, the angular black box whipped forward and cracked into Cikoumas's thin head. He averted his face sharply and went flailing down backward, striking loudly against the floor and the angle of the wall. He lay forever motionless, flung wide.

Michaelmas moved like lightning to the wall. He jumped up to see what Cikoumas had been working. There were incomprehensible knobs and switches in there. He jumped again and snatched the pistol from its cubby. Working at it with both hands, he found the thumb-off for the energizer and the location of the trigger switch. He crouched and faced the white column. Its seams were widening. He stretched out his arms, pointing the pistol. His face convulsed. He turned instead and scrambled to his knees atop the stool, thrust the barrel up above eye level into the control cubby, and fired repeatedly. Clouds of acrid odor poured back into the room. Flame rioted among the sooty shadows, sputtered, and died down. He turned back, half toppling, and kicked the stool aside. The portals were no wider; not much more visible, really, than they had been. The singing had gone with the first shot. Now there was something beginning to bang in there; erratic and disoriented at first, but settling down to a hard rhythmic hammering, like a fist.

Limberg was standing in the doorway, looking. "Send it," Michaelmas said hoarsely, wide-eyed, gesturing, "send it back."

Limberg nodded listlessly and walked slowly to the controls. He looked at them, shook his head, and fumbled in his pockets for a key ring. "I shall have to use the master switches," he said. He went to the opposite wall and unlocked a panel. Michaelmas moved to the center of the floor, holding the pistol and panting. Limberg looked back at him and twitched his mouth. He opened the wall and ran a finger hesitantly along a row of blank circles. He shrugged, finally, and touched two. They and most of the others sprang into green life. One group went red-to-orange-to-yellow, flickering.

"Hurry," Michaelmas said, taking a deep breath.

"I'm not expert at this," Limberg said. He found an

240

alternate subsection by running a forefinger along until he appeared reasonably confident. He pushed hard with all the fingers of his hand, and the cylindrical white cabinet began to sing again. Michaelmas's hands jerked. But the seams were closing; soon they could hardly be seen. The whining came, and then diminished into nothing. The beating and kicking sounds stopped. Michaelmas wiped the back of his hand across his upper lip. "He had me in contact with it long enough, didn't he?" he said. "It was faster than it must have been with Norwood."

"Yes," Limberg said. "Norwood had to be individualized for Fermierla with many, many bits from television documentary recordings. There were many approximations not close enough. Many rejects. In your case, it was possible to present you as a physical model of what was wanted." He began to close the panel. "Is there anything else?"

"Leave it open, Doctor." Michaelmas frowned and cleared his throat. "Leave it open," he tried again, and was better satisfied. He went back to where his headphones still hung from the wall, and started to lift them. He looked at the pistol in his hand, safetied it, and tossed it into the nearest cubby. He slipped the headphones over his ears. There was almost nothing to hear: ". . . sss . . . err . . . masss . . ." and it was very faint. He put one fist around the cord and pulled the jack out, removed the headphones, and laid them gently on the workshelf. He turned to Limberg: "Shut it down. Everything on your end; all the stuff Cikoumas has wired in over the years."

Limberg looked at him, overwhelmed. But he saw something in Michaelmas's face and nodded. He ran his hands over the controls and all of them went steady red. He bowed his head.

241

"I'm in. I'm here," Domino said. "I've got their household systems. Where's the rest?"

"Wait," Michaelmas said. Limberg had left the panel and gone over to where Cikoumas lay. He sat down on the floor beside him and with his fingers began combing the lank hair forward over the wound. He looked up at Michaelmas. "He was attempting to protect humanity," he said. "He couldn't let the astronauts reach Jupiter."

Michaelmas looked back at him. "Why not?"

"That's where the creatures must be. It is the largest, heaviest body in the Solar System, with unimaginable pressures and great electrical potentials. It is a source of radio signals, as everyone knows. Kristiades discussed it with me increasingly after he saw all your broadcasts with the astronauts. 'Such men will find the race of Zusykses,' he said. 'It will be a disaster for us.' And he was right. We are safe from their full attentions only as long as they think we are not real. We must remain hidden among all the accidental systems."

"Yes," Michaelmas said. "Of course."

"He was a brilliant genius!" Limberg declared. "Far worthier than I!"

"He sold out his fathers and his brothers and his sons for a striped suit."

"What will I tell his family?"

"What did you tell them when you said you'd send the grocer's boy to Paris?"

Limberg's upper body rocked back and forth. His eyes closed. "What shall I do with his body?"

"What was he going to do with mine?" Michaelmas began to say. Looking at Limberg, he said instead: "Your systems are being monitored now, and you mustn't touch them. But a

242

little later today, I'll call you, and you can begin to reactivate them step by step under my direction."

"Right," Domino said.

Michaelmas watched Limberg carefully. He said: "When you've reestablished contact with Fermierla, you can shift out this Cikoumas and shift in—"

Limberg's creased cheeks began to run with silent tears.

"For his family," Michaelmas said. He turned to go. "For their sake, find one who's a little easier to get along with, this time."

Limberg stared. "I would not in any case have it want to be here with me. I will send it home to him." He said: "I felt when first you began here with us that you were a messenger of death."

"Domino," Michaelmas said, "get me a cab." He pushed through the door and out into the hall, then along that and past the auditorium, where convalescent ladies and gentlemen were just chattily emerging and discussing the psychically energizing lecture of the therapy professor, and then out through the double doors, and waited outside.

243

Thirteen

He said little to Domino on the ride to the airport, and less on the flight back to New York City. He made sure the Papashvilly interview was going well; otherwise, he initiated nothing, and sat with his chin in his hand, staring at God knew what. From time to time his eyes would attempt to close, but other reflexes and functions in his system would jerk them open again.

From time to time Domino fed him tidbits in an attempt to pique his interest:

"Hanrassy has reneged on her promise to grant EVM an interview." And a little later:

"Westrum's speaking to Hanrassy. Should I patch you in?"

"No. Not unless she takes charge of the conversation."

"She's not."

"That's good enough, then." He thought of that tough,

clever woman on the banks of the Mississippi, putting down her phone and trying to reason out what had happened. She'd alibi to herself eventually—everyone did. She'd decide Norwood and Gately and Westrum were conspiring, somehow, and she'd waste energy trying to find the handle to that. She'd campaign, but she'd be a little off balance. And if it seemed they might still need to play it, there was always the ace in the hole with the income tax official. And that was the end of her. Somewhere among her followers, or in her constituency, was the next person who'd try combining populism and xenophobia. It was a surefire formula that had never in the entire history of American democracy been a winner in the end.

They come and they go, he thought. He rubbed the skin on the backs of his hands, which seemed drier than last year and more ready to fold into diamond-shaped, choppy wrinkles, as if he were a lake with a breeze passing across it.

The EVM crew staked out in Gately's anteroom finally found him consenting to receive them.

"I'd like to take this opportunity to announce to the world," Gately said, "that we are to have the honor, the privilege, and the great personal gratification to welcome Colonel Norwood to these shores on his impending visit." He had changed out of his sweatsuit and was wearing a conservatively cut blue vested pinstripe that set off his waistline when he casually unbuttoned his jacket. He looked almost young enough to go back on active status himself, but his eyes were a little too careful to follow every movement of every member of the interview crew.

Time passed. President Fefre had a mild attack interpreted as indigestion. A man in Paris attempted to leave a flight bag of explosives in the upper elevator of the Eiffel Tower, but police alerted by a fortuitous tap into a political conversation arrested him promptly. Another man, in Florence, was found to have embezzled a huge amount of money from the funds of the provincial lottery. He was the brother of the provincial governor; it seemed likely that there would be heightened public disillusion in that quarter of the nation. Rome, which had been a little dilatory in its supervision, would have to be a bit more alert for some time, so who was to say there was not some good in almost anything? And most of the money was recovered. Also, a small private company in New Mexico, composed of former engineering employees striking out on their own, applied for a patent on an engine featuring half the energy consumption of anything with comparable output. The president of the company and his chief engineer had originally met while coincidentally booked into adjoining seats on an intercity train. Meanwhile, a hitherto insignificant individual in Hamburg ran his mother-in-law through the eye with a fork at his dinner table, knocked down his wife, went to the waterfront, attempted clumsily to burn his father-in-law's warehouse, and professed honestly to have lost all memory of any of these preceding events when he was found sitting against a bollard and crying with the hoarse persistence of a baby while staring out over the water. But not all of this was reported to Michaelmas immediately. Domino thought and thought on what the world might be like when a completely even tenor had settled over all its policies, and there was nothing left for the news to talk about but the incessant, persistent, perhaps rising sound of individual people demanding to assert their existence.

Two trains were inadvertently switched onto the same track in Holland. But another switch, intended to stay closed, opened fortuitously, and the freight slid out of the path of the holiday passenger express.

In the systems of the Limberg Sanatorium, there was nothing overt.

"All right, then," Domino said, "if you don't want to listen, will you talk? What happened at the sanatorium? Limberg's keeping everybody out of the room with Cikoumas's body, seeing no one, sitting in his office, and obviously waiting for someone to tell him what to do next."

Michaelmas grunted. He said: "Well, they were laboratory curiosities and the person in charge of them is sentimental and intrigued. When they proposed something ingenious, such as moving something coherent from one arbitrary frame of reference into a highly similar frame, they were indulged. Why not? The experiment may be trivial, or it may be taken as proof that there are no orders of greater or lesser likelihood among sets, but in either case it was suggested by a member of the experiment. You have to admit that would intrigue almost anyone, let alone a poet in heat." Michaelmas smiled as though something had struck his mouth like a riding whip. "Poke around, now that you're inside Limberg's system. Open one part of the circuitry at a time. You'll meet what's been chasing you. Be careful to keep a firm hold on the switching."

There was a pause. Then the machine was back. "It . . . it seems we here are considered an effect." Domino paused again.

"We are an effect," Michaelmas said. "They have a means of scanning infinity. When they want a model of an elephant, they tune out everything that doesn't look like an elephant. When they deduce there's a human race, they get a human race. Warts and all. The difference between the model of the elephant and the human race is that the representatives of that race can speak; they can request, and they can propose. They can even believe they think they represent *the* human race. But in all of infinity, the chances are infinite that they are only drifting particles."

He said nothing more for a long time, blinking like an owl in the bright midafternoon sunshine of Long Island, looking a little surprised when his bag was put aboard his cab for him.

In the apartment, he sat at the desk, he brooded out the window, he tuned his guitar, and then a lute, and a dulcimer. Finally he began to be able to speak, and spoke to Domino in a slow, careful voice, pausing to marshal his facts and to weight them in accord with their importance to the narrative.

He barely listened to himself explaining. He sat and thought:

> *I cannot find you.*
> *At proper seasons I can hear*
> *The migrant voices as the flocks in air*
> *Move north or south against the sun,*
> *They come, they go, they move as one,*
> *and darken briefly.*
> *I cannot find you.*

"So that was it?" Domino asked. "Mere scientific curiosity? This Fermierla contacted Limberg at some point in the past—Well, why not? They must have been very much alike, at one time; yes, I can see the sense in that—and then Limberg began to see ways in which this could be useful, but it was after he brought in Cikoumas that the enterprise began to accelerate. Fermierla still thinking it was in touch with fantasy creatures—"

"Not in touch. Not . . . in touch."

"In contact with. And Medlimb prospered. But Cikoumas became worried; suppose UNAC found Fermierla? Suppose Doktor Limberg was exposed to the world for what he was, and Cikoumas with him. But that's all unrealistic. Fermierla's no more on Jupiter than I am. These biological people are all scientific illiterates, rife with superstition. You tell them radio signals, and they think WBZ. They have no idea of the scale of what's involved here. They—"

"Yes, yes," Michaelmas said. "Take over Limberg, will you? Manage the rest of his life for him. Meanwhile, there's one more thing I have to do before I can end this day."

"Yes, I suppose," Domino said, and put in a call to Clementine Gervaise, who was in Paris. Michaelmas squeezed his hands and punched up full holo; she sat at a desk within a few feet of him, a pair of eyeglasses pushed up into her hair, her lipstick half worn off her lower lip, and a hand-editiing machine beside the desk.

"Laurent," she said, "it is good to have you call, but you catch me at a devil of a time." She smiled suddenly. "Nevertheless, it is good to have you call." The smile was fleetingly very young. "From New York." Now she appeared a little downcast. "You departed from Europe very quickly."

"I didn't expect you in Paris. I thought you'd still be in Africa."

She shook her head. "We have a problem," she said. She turned to the editor, flicked fingers over the keyboard with offhand dexterity, and gestured: "See there."

A sequence aboard the UNAC executive plane came up.

Norwood was smiling and talking. The point of view changed to a reverse angle closeup of Douglas Campion asking a question. As he spoke, his forehead suddenly swelled, then returned to normal, but his eyes lengthened and became slits while the bridge of his nose seemed to valley into his skull. Next his mouth enlarged, and his chin shrank. Finally the ripple passed down out of sight, but another began at the top of his head, while he spoke on obliviously.

"We can't get it out," Clementine said. "It happens in every shot of Campion. We've checked the computer, we've checked our mixers." She shrugged. "I suppose someone will say we should check this editor, too, now. But we are either going to have to scrap the entire program or substitute another interviewer."

"Can't you get hold of Campion and reshoot him?"

She made an embarrassed little face. "I think he is overdrawn at his bank, or something of that sort. He cannot get validation for an airplane seat. Not even his telephone works," she said. She blushed slightly. "I am in a little trouble for recommending that sort of person."

"Oh, come, Clementine, you're not seriously worried about that. Not with your talent. However, that is amazing about Campion. He seems to be having a run of bad luck."

"Well, this isn't why you called me," she said. She waved a hand in dismissal behind her. "Either that works or it doesn't; tomorrow comes anyway. You're right." She rested her elbows on her desktop and cupped her face in her hands, looking directly at him: "Tell me—what is it you wish with me?"

"Well, I just wanted to see how you were," he said slowly. "I rushed off suddenly, and—"

251

"Ah, it's the business. Whatever you went for, I suppose you got it. And I suppose the rest of us will hear about it on the news."

"Not—not this time, I'm afraid."

"Then it was personal."

"I suppose." He was having trouble. "I just wanted to say 'Hello.' "

She smiled. "And I would like to say it to you. When are you next in Europe?"

He took a breath. It was hard to do. He shrugged. "Who knows?" He found himself beginning to tremble.

"I shall be making periodic trips to North America very soon, I think. I could even request doing coverage of Norwood's US tour. It starts in a few days. It's only an overnight wonder, but if we move it quickly, there will still be interest." She cocked an eyebrow. "Eh? What do you think? We could be together in a matter of days."

He thrust back convulsively in his chair. "I—ah—call me," he managed. "Call me when it's definite. If I can. . . ." He squirmed. She began to frown and to tilt her head the slightest bit to one side, as if gazing through a shop window at a hat that had seemed more cunning from a little farther away. ". . . if I'm here," he was saying, he realized.

"Yes, Laurent," she said sadly. "We must keep in touch."

In the night for many years, he would from time to time say the word "touch" distinctly, without preamble, and thrust up his arms toward his head, but this was not reported to him.

"Au' voir."

"Au revoir, Clementine." He ended the call, and sat for a while.

"Well," Domino said, "now you know how you feel."

Michaelmas nodded. "She may readily have been given only conventional treatment at the sanatorium. But, yes, now we know how I feel."

"I could check the records."

"Like you checked their inventories."

"Now that I'm situated in their covert hardware, I'm quite confident I can assimilate any tricks in their soft mechanisms. I can run a real check."

"Yes," Michaelmas said sadly. "Run a real check on infinity."

"Well. . . ."

"Life's too short," Michaelmas said.

"Yours?"

"No." Michaelmas stretched painfully, feeling the knotted muscles and grimacing at the swollen taste of his tongue. He worked the bed and began undressing. Somewhere out beyond his windows, a helicopter buffeted by on some emergency errand. He shook his head and closed his eyes momentarily. He opened them long enough to pull back the coverlet. "No calls," he said, darkening the windows. "Not for eight hours; longer if possible." He lay down, pulling the cover up over the hunch of his shoulder, putting his left hand on his right wrist and his right hand under his cheek. He settled himself. "It's one good feature of this occupation," he remarked in a voice that trailed away. "I never have any trouble getting to sleep."